Righteous Gangsta

Rise of the Blac Angel

Erick Williams

ONE

Reverend Stephon Reed approaches the oak wood podium, smiling as he gazes at the congregation. He has been part of the New Beginnings Methodist Church for over fifteen years. Standing 5'7" with a pot belly and a slender frame, he sports the George Jefferson hairstyle, a small afro that's balding in the center. Dressed in his full-length purple robe, the Reverend appears regal. Standing directly in front of the microphone, he confidently announces, "Here is a selection from our Choir." He then turns to the choir director, nodding in acknowledgment, who rises, faces the twenty-five-member choir, and signals them to stand with his right hand. They all wear matching robes in the same shade as the Reverend's. Sage Reed, the pastor's 25-year-old son, nervously stands up. He is also 5'7" and slender with short wavy hair and black stud earrings. He steps forward to take the microphone. The director waves his hand, and the music begins playing over the church sound system: "Old Happy Day." He sings with the choir, harmonizing behind him. His voice resembles that of R&B singer Johnny Gill. He starts nervously slowly. An older lady in the front pew notices his nervousness. She quickly stands up and enthusiastically claps to encourage him.

She loudly shouts, "You got it, Brother Sage! Let the spirit lead you."

He smiles at her now, feeling the music flowing through him, and is all in. Inspired by her spirit, he becomes more confident and fully engaged, jumping and clapping, selling out for the Lord. While singing, he notices a beautiful woman he hasn't seen before, recording him with her phone. Sage tries not to get caught staring. Now fully engaged at the song's crescendo, over half the church is dancing, clapping, and stomping. The church is filled with the spirit and heat. With all the dancing and shouting, the air conditioning is working overtime to keep up. After about ten minutes, the music fades into the closing, and people sit down and yell spontaneously, "Amen, Praise the Lord!" Wooooo! Brother Sage, you are gifted!" He looks at the fine sister, who is still recording and clapping. He smiles at her, puts the microphone back on the podium, and sits down. He thinks to himself, *I gotta meet her.*

The Reverend returns and steps to the pulpit, leans into the microphone yells, "Praise God! It is indeed a Happy Day! Thank you, choir, and a special thanks to my talented son." He turns to his right and looks at him. Then taps his right fist on his chest over his heart. Sage responds with the same gesture.

The Reverend opens his bible and says, "Today's sermon comes from Matthew 16:26. If you will turn your bible....

Following the church service, Sage promptly changes out of his robe in the choir room. He hurries to meet the woman who was recording him earlier before she leaves.

He rushes down the hall, receiving a few congratulations from church members on his performance. In the sanctuary, he spots her talking to another lady, her back turned to him. He swiftly approaches from behind. When her friend notices him, she points, prompting the woman to turn quickly.

She smiles at him, extends her right hand, and greets him, "Good afternoon, brother. I'm Candace Day. I work in the music industry." She pulls a business card from her phone case.

He takes the card, reads it, and mutters, "**Candace Day, A&R Scout.**" He then looks back at her, staring for a few seconds, visibly stunned by her beauty. She stands about 5'9", slightly taller than him. Her skin is a smooth, dark chocolate tone. Her hair is jet black, straightened just past her shoulders. She wears small silver cross earrings and a matching cross necklace.

She looks at him, "Yes. Have you ever thought about singing professionally?"

Surprised by the question, he stutters, "No, I just sing for my church."

He looks at the other lady, who states, "I'm Shanice Jacobson, her older sister. I'm not in the industry; I come for the service and to keep her company."

He notices the family resemblance. She is just as beautiful; Shanice's hair is also jet black and cornrowed, flipped to the right side of her head. She is wearing more makeup and has dimples when she smiles. He mumbles, "A music producer, humph."

Candace interrupts him, "Yes, I am visiting different churches, looking for new gospel talent. I'm trying to put together a compilation of singers. I saw your performance today and was inspired. Have you ever thought about pursuing music?"

"No. I'm not fond of singing; the Reverend insists I do it. I get nervous singing in front of a lot of people."

He smiles at her and takes his shot, "Maybe we can talk about it over dinner tonight."

Candace catches the hint, snaps back, "Probably not."

"Sage! Sage! We need to talk." A female voice hollers out to him.

He cringes at the sound of the voice. It's Amira, his six-year-old son Aiden's mom.

Annoyed, he turns around and sees her strutting towards him.

She and Sage are the same height. Her complexion is lighter than Candace's and Shanice's.

She looks good, but her outfit is not church-appropriate. It's a skin-tight yellow long-sleeve tee, with a skin-tight skirt, and a pair of white platform tennis shoes. He asks, "What do you want? Can't you see I'm busy?"

"I don't care. We need to talk."

"Can we do this later?"

"No, I'm busy later." She pauses, eyeballs Candace and Shanice up and down, then smartly replies, "Well, since we're all here, we can talk."

Candace and Shanice look at each other uncomfortably. Candace answers, "That's okay, you got my card." They both walk away.

"Alright. What you want? He looks around for his son. "Where is Aiden?"

"He's still in children's church. I need two bills for your son."

He chuckles to himself, "Do you need or want it?"

"What difference does it make? Let me get it, and I'll be out."

He pulls out his wallet, riffles through a few bills, and gives her the money.

She snatches the bills, folds them, and puts them inside her left bra strap. "If I knew you were holding like that, I would have gotten more."

He puts his wallet away and replies, "No, you wouldn't." She prances away as quickly as she came. He watches her leave and wonders how he got caught up with someone like her. He walks to the front doors of the nearly empty church.

The Reverend and his mom, Sydney, are at the doors saying goodbye to the remaining parishioners.

“Beautiful selection today, son. That voice of yours is a special gift.”

“Thank you, Reverend.”

The Reverend continues, “I want to talk with you later.”

Sage already knows what he wants to discuss, and walking to his car without looking back, he yells, “I'll see you at the house.”

TWO

Sage still lives with his parents in a modest two-story brick house with beige shutters on each of the four windows. His son, Aiden, runs down the stairs and hugs his right leg as he comes inside.

Happily, he yells, “Hi, Daddy. What you doing here?”

Aiden holds on as Sage walks stiff-legged to the couch. He responds, “I live here. The real question is, what are you doing here?”

Sage sits down as Aiden gets off his leg and sits on the couch beside him.

Sage’s mom, Sydney, enters the living room from the kitchen. She is 5’5” with brown skin like Sage’s. Her shoulder-length crochet braids complement her slim, athletic build. She enjoys working out and eating healthy. She and Aiden were frosting cupcakes they had baked earlier, before church.

She beams with joy as she watches Sage gently tickle Aiden on the couch. It truly warms her heart to see him happily spending quality time with his son.

“We are about to go to a birthday party at Ducky’s Pizza as soon as I pack these cupcakes.” She announces.

She goes back to the kitchen as Aiden's laughter echoes through the room. From there, she calls out, "Sage, let him go get his shoes."

He stops tickling him, and Aiden runs up the stairs. After five minutes, he returns wearing white tennis shoes on the wrong feet. Sage sees this and tells him, "Come here, son, your shoes are on the wrong feet."

As Sage fixes his shoes, Sydney enters the living room with a Tupperware container full of chocolate buttercream cupcakes.

He finishes tying his shoe. Aiden runs over to his mee-maw. "What time y'all coming back?" Sage questions.

"We not. After the party, I'm taking him home to Amira."

Sage gets up and hugs Aiden, "All right, son, I will see you next week."

They leave, and the house becomes peaceful and quiet. He relaxes on the couch, leans back comfortably, and gently closes his eyes. Ten seconds later.

"Sage. Come in here." A deep voice beckons.

The Reverend calls from his study.

Sage takes a deep breath, feeling anxiety and frustration. He exhales, slaps his hands on his knees, and then stands up.

He goes to the study. It is a small, dimly lit room with no windows. The Reverend sits behind a vast wooden desk in a giant black leather chair akin to a throne. He is typing on a laptop. Behind him is a bookshelf full of books. There is a smaller matching black leather chair in front of his desk.

“Take a seat.” He gestures to the chair.

Sage pulls the chair away from the desk and sits down. The Reverend stops typing and closes his laptop. He takes a deep breath and sighs, “Have you thought any more about what we discussed?”

“Reverend, I have, and I don’t feel ready. I’m not sure I will ever be.”

“Son, when I dedicated my life entirely to Christ, I was uncertain of my readiness; however, your mother supported me throughout this journey. Have faith in the Lord. Psalm 55:22. Cast your burdens on the LORD, and He will sustain you.”

Sage isn't swayed by the scripture smirks and answers, "Look, I have a lot going on right now. I just don't have the time.”

"Ye shall never suffer the righteous to be moved.”

The Reverend gets up from behind the desk, walks around, sits on the corner, and leans in on Sage aggressively, “You think I’m stupid? Ignorant? I hear what you’re doing out in the streets. You don’t have to follow the old adage of the preacher's kid being the worst.”

Protesting loudly, he quickly springs up, causing the Rev to have to jerk back to avoid being hit. Sage leans down at him and shouts in anger, “I’m a grown man; I do what I want!”

The Reverend's voice erupts with fury, "I look like a hypocrite! Every Sunday, I stand here preaching the word, while you sing in the choir! And then, that same night, you're out on the streets all night peddling that poison! Have you ever stopped to think about what that makes me look like?"

Upset about being called out by his father, “I don’t give a damn! I don’t tell you how to live your life! Don’t tell me how to live mine!” He storms out of the study.

The reverend follows behind, “Get back here! Don’t walk away from me when I’m talking to you!”

Without breaking stride, Sage ignores him and continues to the front door.

The Reverend wanders into the hallway and screams, “You going to have to make a choice! You can’t serve two masters!”

THREE

Sage hears the Reverend's comment, snickers at it, and thinks, *Whatever, man, I need my own place. I'm done with him preaching to me all the time.*

Outside on the front porch, he sits on the white patio chair, leans back, closes his eyes, inhales deep breaths, and tries to relax. He enjoys the sun on his face and the quietness of the moment.

Needing to get away, he spontaneously jumps up and gets in his black Lexus sports coupe. His business phone is in the center console. 'Q,' his gang leader has texted him *come to the spot.*

He texts back, 'On my way.' The 'spot' is the trap house where they run their business. He keeps driving past the torn-up duplexes and row houses. Every corner has a liquor store, convenience store, or pawn shop. The sidewalks are busy with people wearing AirPods, staring at their phones. He turns right and drives through a residential area with more homes on both sides. At the street's end, there's a cul-de-sac. He pulls to the right and parks before the 'spot.'

It's a single-story, gray wooden house with an attached garage. Every window has metal bars. The front door has a metal gate, and the door is metal. As Sage exits his car, he grabs his backpack. Four-bangers are outside, talking and joking with each other. He gives them the quick 'what's up' head bob. Sage walks to the front door and puts in the code. The door clicks open, and a raggedy blue pleather couch facing a fake fireplace is in the living room. To the left of the sofa is an old white plastic eight-foot-long table facing a wall. It has two brown folding metal chairs in front of it. A blue-and-yellow bong is on the table, and some rolled-up five-to-ten-band. Some weed buds are also scattered out on the table. Sage sits and starts to fill the bong with some of the buds. He hears the toilet flush, and a 6'1" muscular caramel-colored bro enters the kitchen a few seconds later. Q is an ex-Marine. He is thirty-five years old. Q served for over 10 years and completed two tours of duty in the Middle East. He was dishonorably discharged for bad conduct. He has long blond dreadlocks that hang down his back. '187' in Old English font is tattooed on his right forearm. His hair and full black beard make a dynamic contrast.

He sits beside Sage at the table. They dap up with the 187 handshake.

"What's up, my boy Big Saint?" Big Saint is Sage's nickname in the hood.

"What's good? Check this, I have a proposition for you."

Sage looks at him, interested. "What's up?"

"We're expanding. We got 187 on lockdown and will take over Graham next."

Big Saint's excited but maintains his cool, "Aight, bet. What you need me to do?"

"It's yours. You and Kong run it. We are about to set up another trap on Graham. I texted Kong; he should be pulling up soon."

Kong is an enforcer/bodyguard of the '187'. He and Sage are high school boys. Sage set up Kong with the 187's after graduation.

Q stands up, goes to his room, and returns with two mason jars full of buds.

He drops them on the table. He enters the kitchen and returns with a big steel mixing bowl and a box of plastic sandwich bags.

Q sits down at the table. "Let's get ready for tonight."

He opens the jars and pours the buds into the giant bowl. They start sifting through the buds, breaking them up, and pulling out the stems.

Q opens the box of plastic bags and puts some buds in them. He places the bag on the scale. They are making bags of 1/8 oz for $30 and 1/4 oz for $60. After they are weighed, they are rolled up, and a rubber band is placed around the bag. Any leftover leaves are rolled up into joints.

As they continue to sift through the buds, the front door opens. Kong steps into the trapt.

Kong's real name is Cameron King. He got the nickname from his high school football days. With his 6'5" 250 lbs. size, he is used to intimidating people. He played defensive end in football. He had a few scholarship offers, but tore his ACL in the first game of his senior year of high school. He got burned out rehabbing from the injury. He doesn't like the gang lifestyle and is considering getting back into football to try to get a college scholarship.

Kong enters the house, Q and Big Saint stand up and exchange dap and the 187 handshake with him. Kong looks at Q. "I got a couple of bags in my truck. Let's go get them."

Q goes to his room and comes back with his Glock 9 mm. He racks the slide back to chamber a round.

He holds it down to his side, "All right, let's go."

Kong walks out to his blue Ford truck. Q stands by the truck, scanning the area, while Sage waits at the door.

Kong unlocks the truck, reaches onto the back floor, and brings out two plastic bags of weed, each weighing a pound. He shuffles to the house as Q walks backward, covering his six. Once inside, Q takes the bags to his room and secures them in a safe underneath his bed.

When he returns, Big Saint and Kong are at the table bagging the weed. Kong looks up at Q and inquires, "What's the deal with Graham?"

FOUR

Q walks over to the front door and looks at the sun fading in the afternoon sky.

“We're blowing up, bros, and I figure now is a good time to make a move, you know, grow the empire. We set up Graham next week. Start slow and see how business flows, and take it from there.”

“What’s our cut?” Big Saint asks as he starts putting the bags in his backpack.

“I’m thinking twenty to start. Once we get it up and running smoothly, it will increase.”

“Is the trap on Graham going to run like this?” Kong asks.

“Graham is smaller, so it will be a satellite post. This will be the headquarters, the base of operations. Graham will be a spot where you can restock, and the hoes can do their business.”

He turns around and looks at them, “What you think?”

Big Saint and Kong look at each other. Kong shrugs, “Bro, let me think about it.”

Q, upset with his answer, yells, “What's to think about? This is a big opportunity. I thought you would be the one to jump on this!”

Still angry, he looks at Big Saint, “What about you?” He takes a deep breath and thinks about his father's talk. He can get his own space with that money. “Yeah, I’ll give it a shot.”

Q excitedly walks over to him and daps him up, “Bet! That’s what I’m talking about, boy!”

“Now get out there and make me some money!”

<<<<>>>>

Big Saint drives while Kong is in the passenger seat. His phone is hooked up, blasting some hip-hop. He looks at Kong and yells over the music, “You good, dawg?”

The question confuses him, so he turns down the music.

“Yeah, fool, why you ask?” Kong answers

“Honestly, I thought you would be all in for Graham.”

“I don’t know, bro. I know it sounds good. It's just...

Kong's phone rings through his AirPods. He pulls it out of his gray hoodie. It’s his four-year-old son, Luke.

He is Face Timing with Luke as he waves, “Hi, Daddy.”

Kong waves back at him, answers, “Hey, Luke. What ya doing?”

“Me and Mommy just watched a movie. It’s bedtime, so mommy, let me call you to say goodnight.”

Kong stares at the phone, smiling, "Good night, little man." He kisses his two fingers and blows the kiss toward the phone, "Love ya."

His baby momma, Brigette, gets on the phone, "Love you, Cameron. See you later."

Big Saint turns left into a small convenience store and parks on the left side of the building. He is careful to pick an inconspicuous spot, yet he can still keep an eye on his car.

Kong knows it's time to go to work. "Love you, girl." He ends the FaceTime.

"Alright, let's do this." Big Saint remarks as he opens the car door and grabs his backpack.

Kong puts his cell phone in the glove box, grabs the Glock, and puts it in the hoodie's pocket.

They walk to the corner with Big Saint in front, and Kong follows about five feet back.

"Yo, Big Saint! Hold up!" An unknown man quickly comes up from behind.

Kong turns to his right and puts out his right arm to stop the man. "Yo homey, what you doing?"

The dude stops and raises both his hands to show he poses no threat. "It's cool; it's cool. Just want some green."

Kong looks down at him, “Nigga you know better than to be running up on us.”

Sage walks around Kong with a calmer tone, “I got the trees you need. What you want?” He pulls out an eighth bag and daggles it before him, “That’s thirty, my boy.”

The man pulls out a twenty with two fives.

Kong snatches the bills as Big Saint gives him the bag.

The man stuffs it in the right back pocket of his jeans and shuffles back to his car.

They continue walking to the corner and post in their usual position, Big Saint right out front on the corner. Kong is ten feet behind, watching his back. There is no time for talk between the druggies, prostitutes, and cops. It’s best if you keep your head on a swivel. When a customer comes by, he directs them to the parking lot. He saunters up to the driver's side door. His first line is, “I got the trees you want, eighths or quarters.” Kong is always in the cut, surveying the scene. He tracks the sales on the burner. After each sale, he yells to Kong, either ‘eighth’ or ‘quarter.’

A small, beat-up red car parks next to Big Saint’s. Three hours in, they are both on the corner, trying to get rid of the last couple of bags. The horn starts blowing, catching both of their attention. Kong, being closer, walks over to the car. The window comes down as he walks over to the driver's door.

A disheveled, heavy-set woman pokes her head out, “Can I get four blunts?”

Kong looks up from the window, “Yo, you got a customer.”

Big Saint shuffles up. He comes to the door as Kong steps back. “What ya need?”

The woman looks up at him, smiling, and replies, “Four blunts.”

He turns his bag around and unzips the small front pocket, “I got what you need. That’s twenty.”

“Umm, I’m a little short at the moment. Can we work something out?”

She stares at his crotch and starts applying some cherry red lipstick.

He zips up the bag's front and looks back at Kong. He turns to the woman, laughing loudly, “Hell no, I’m good. This is a cash business, either that paper or those apps.”

She grabs his right hand. “C’mon, honey, it will be the best head you ever had.”

Kong steps over and grabs the woman's dirty hand from on top of Big Saint’s. She looks at Kong, “I’ll do both of you right behind the store.”

Kong, in a deep, threatening voice, “You heard my man. If you don’t have either, keep it moving.”

They both walk away. She starts her car. As she backs out, she shouts, “Fuck you, punks! You don’t know what you missed.”

They both laugh. Big Saint states, “I’m tired of fools trying to get handouts. I’m done, bro.” He goes to the car.

They are driving back to the trap to drop off their gear.

“What do you think about Graham?” Big Saint inquires.

“I didn’t say anything to Q, but I’m trying to escape this life. I don’t want to be doing this forever. In a few weeks, I’m going down to Andrew State to talk to the coaches about walking on and hopefully even getting a scholarship.”

Big Saint looks over at him, his eyes wide with excitement, “Bet, bro, I’m happy for you.”

“Preciate it. I’m giving it my best shot. This could be my way out.”

Big Saint replies, “I got some news myself. I had some hot music producer come up to me after church, talking about wanting to sign me.”

“That’s cool, Big Saint. What did you say?”

“I didn’t say anything, bro. I just got her card today. I haven’t had a chance to reach out yet.”

Kong excitedly responds, “Fool, what you waiting for? This could be your chance!”

Big Saint, irritated by his tone, "Chill down, bro. I only met her today. I'm not even sure I will reach out. She came off a little big time. Chuckling, he adds, "She is fine, though."

They pull up to the trap and park behind Kong's truck.

"You need to follow through. This could be your shot. You don't want to do this forever, do you?"

Big Saint reaches back into the backseat, opens the bag, and grabs a handful of money. "Bro, we just cleared five hundred tax-free in three hours. I'm good. What I don't want to be is some lawn jockey cutting grass in the heat for eight hours. Doing the nine-to-five ain't the life I want."

Kong shakes his head no, "Between these crazy hours, worrying about other sets rolling up on you, and the popo, I know this ain't the life. I got Luke and Brigette to think about. You said she was fine. Why don't you hit her up and see what's up?"

Big Saint gets his gear out of the car, "Aight, bro, whatever. It's late. I need to get home. I gotta lawn jockey in the morning."

FIVE

Sage pushes the lawnmower up the ramp into the back of the Reverend's red quad cab truck. They have been mowing since eight this morning. It's now almost five-thirty. He wipes sweat from his forehead with a red bandana as the sun starts to set. Sage is both tired and hungry. He secures the lawnmower with the black rubber straps. The Reverend is inside the truck with the air conditioner on full blast, enjoying a bottle of water. Sage gets in and adjusts the vents so they blow directly in his face. The Reverend puts the truck in drive and takes off. He looks at Sage and remarks, "This heat ain't no joke."

Sage reaches into the back seat, grabs a water, and starts chugging. He shakes his head to acknowledge the comment. His phone pings in the truck's passenger door console. He hears it but does not want to check it while his father is there. After finishing the bottle, he answers, "Yeah, it's been brutal all summer."

They pull into a convenience store gas station. The Rev gets out of the truck and instructs Sage, "I need to get some gas for the mowers and truck. Fill up the truck first."

"Cool."

Sage watches as he walks into the store. He then grabs his phone.

Candace texted him, *Have you thought about our conversation?*

He thinks back to the talk he and Kong had last night. He nods to himself and texts back, I'm interested, *can we meet?"*

He looks up from his phone and sees Stephon waiting in line. He puts the phone back in the console and goes to the pump. The Reverend walks out to the truck and gets in. Sage starts to fill it up. The Reverend listens to gospel on the radio. Sage pulls the two red five-gallon gas cans from the back of the truck. Stephon opens the window and yells, "Don't forget the receipt." Sage shakes his head to acknowledge him.

On the drive home, the Reverend casually mentions, "I'm not trying to have any problems, but have you thought any more about what we talked about?"

Sage chuckles and breathes deeply, "We had a good day, Dad, and I don't want any drama, either. It is best if we don't talk about it."

In a stern voice, the Rev responds, "This is my final word on it… for now. Burying your head in the sand does not make it go away."

If you keep pushing, you probably won't like where this ends, he thinks, but keeps it to himself.

Instead, he shakes his head in agreement.

Switching it up, “You got any plans tonight?” The Reverend asks.

“This heat wore me out. I’m taking a shower, getting something to eat, and chilling.” Sage answers as he yawns.

The Reverend smiles and answers, “That doesn’t sound like a bad idea.”

Sage relaxes with his eyes closed as the radio plays and the a/c blows.

<<<<>>>>

Q knocks three times on the green wooden door. He can hear the TV playing a kids' cartoon show. He impatiently checks the time on his phone. He pounds on the door with the side of his right fist three more times.

“Yo Kong!” he yells.

Kong comes to the door carrying his son in his right arm. The boy is biting his nails. He is a little mini Kong.

Q nervously peeks into the apartment and looks around, “Yo, anybody else here?”

“Naw, dawg, just me, and Luke. Come in.”

He puts Luke down, and he stands beside him, next to Kong’s left leg. Kong reaches around Q and shuts the door.

"Take a seat, bro," he points to a brown leather couch on the other side of the room.

Kong sits in an old green recliner that does not match the room. He grabs the remote from the side pocket of the recliner and turns the TV down. Luke runs up to him and jumps on his lap.

He points at Q, "Daddy, who's that?"

Kong pulls his hand down and answers, "That's a friend of daddy's. Can you get your iPad? I need to talk to him for a few minutes." Luke jumps off his lap and runs out of the living room.

Q looks at him as he runs away, "Cute kid." He then turns to Kong, leans into him, and whispers, "I got a mission for you."

"What's up?"

Still in a low voice, "We talked about moving in on Graham. We do it next week. We expanding and need more product to cover everything. I need my main man to go to New Elk City and pick up ten pounds. Everything is taken care of."

He stares back at Q and thinks about the talk he and Big Saint had, wondering if he should let Q know what's on his mind.

Q continues, "I'll get you some extra in your account to make it worth your time."

Kong slowly shakes his head, mulling it over, and inquires, "Everything's taken care of? All I'm doing is picking up and delivering, right? What day we talking?"

"It's covered, bro. I want this mission to be as discreet as possible. I need someone I can depend on, someone I trust. That's why I'm giving it to you. This stays in the family. It's happening this weekend. I will text you the address later. You in?"

"Yeah, bro, I got you." He leans forward towards Q, and they do the 187 dap.

Q gets up from the couch and heads to the door. "Aight, dawg, I'll get back with you."

Kong follows behind him and opens the door. Brigette is standing there, fumbling for her keys, surprising both of them.

Flustered by her appearance, Kong mumbles, "What's up, Jet?"

Q steps outside. Jet looks at Q disgustedly and mutters, "Humph." She walks into the house. Luke runs up and hugs her. Brigette bends down and returns the hug. They walk to the kitchen.

Q sensing the awkwardness, "Alright, bro, we'll talk." They bro hug, and Q whispers, "187 for life." After Kong comes back inside, Brigette is waiting at the door.

"What's he doing here?" She demands.

"Just talking some business." He answers as he steps around her, goes to the recliner, and sits down.

"Did you tell him you're getting out?"

"No. It wasn't a good time. I got this one last job, then I'm out. I promise."

She walks up to him and kneels down to get at eye level. With a determined look and tone, she tells him, "If you don't, then Luke and I are leaving." He looks at her serious expression but doesn't respond. She gets up and walks to the kitchen.

Later, that night in bed, Sage's phone pings beside him. It's a text from Candace: *Got your text. Sorry for not answering sooner. I'm not in town, but I should be back this weekend. We can get together then.*

He puts his phone back on the nightstand and lies back down with a slight smile.

SIX

Sage is driving home from choir practice when a text from Candace pops up: "*I made it home earlier today." I would love to be treated to a good dinner at Sal's.*

He chuckles as he reads it, shakes his head, and speaks out loud, *Sal's? Never been there now, I got a reason. What time works for you?* Send."

He was going to go to the corner for a few hours with Kong, but was excited for the opportunity to finally meet up with Candace.

He calls Kong after a few rings. He picks up,

"Yo, Big Saint, What's up?"

"That producer wants to have a date at Sal's."

"I hear you. You going?"

"Come on, dawg. You need to ask. She just texted me a few minutes ago, giving you the heads up that I won't be out tonight."

"Bet Big Saint, I'll probably go by the trap later to see what's popping. Don't blow it, fool." Kong hangs up.

Sage pulls into the driveway of his house.

Right after, an incoming call message pops up on his screen.

He answers, and Candace blurts out, “What up? Is tonight good for you?”

Surprised by her confidence, “Umm, sure, eight is good. Do you want me to pick you up at seven?”

“No. I’ll meet you there at eight. See you tonight. Don’t be late.” She commands.

<<<<>>>>

Sage has showered and changed into some fresh gear. He hops down the stairs quickly, and his mom yells, “Going out?”

The Reverend and Sydney are in the kitchen at the table, playing a game of chess. Sydney yells from the kitchen, “Where are you going, sweetheart?”

He walks into the kitchen wearing a stand-collar red polka-dot long-sleeve button-down shirt, black slim-cut slacks, and is bathed in cologne.

Smiling, she says, “Looking good. Who’s the lady?”

“Candace, I met her after church last week. She heard me in the choir and is interested in producing me.”

“That’s great. Why didn’t you tell us?”

“We only talked for a few minutes after church. I’m feelin her out, nothing to get excited about yet.”

The Reverend is quiet the whole time, snarkily replies, “Hopefully, she’ll give you a reason to get off the streets.”

Hearing the disdain in his comment, Sage glares at him, quickly turns and walks away, and yells, “Goodnight, mom.” He slams the door as he leaves.

She looks over the table at him and sighs, “Why have you always got to be so spiteful to him?”

“I’m just trying to make a man out of him.”

I know he ain’t living the life you envisioned for him, but he’s still young. There is still time for him to come around. You’re his father, you can’t give up on him.”

“How can I have faith in him if he doesn’t have faith in me?”

“You are a pastor; doesn’t the bible say, ‘Hatred stirs up dissension, but love covers all wrong.’

“That’s a fair point, but it also says, ‘Refuse to let the world corrupt you.’ Which is obviously happening to him.”

She looks at him disgustedly and sweeps her left hand across the board, knocking down the chess pieces. She gets up from the game without saying another word.

“I see where he gets his attitude from!” He yells.

<<<<<>>>>>

Sage pulls into the parking lot of Sal’s. The lot is only half full, so that he can park on the right, next to the restaurant. He is nervous and anxious as he exits the car and sprints to the restaurant. When he enters the front lobby, he is surprised to see Candace discreetly sitting on a wooden bench, taking a selfie on her phone.

Surprised, he asks, “How long you been here?”

She stands up and gives him a warm, friendly hug. Tells him, “In my profession, if you're ten minutes early, you’re late. If we're going to do business, you need to remember that.”

The waitress's stand is empty. There is a sign on it that reads. **You can seat yourself.**

Walking to the table, she assertively takes the lead, following as he checks out her drip. Her outfit is a solid apricot-ice short-sleeve crew-neck dress with matching all-white basketball shoes.

The restaurant is lit dimly, nearly empty, with blue tablecloths and candles on each table. They go to a corner booth. A young blond-haired male waiter approaches.

“Good evening, welcome to Sal’s. Can I get you a beverage?”

“Let me get a glass of Cabernet Sauvignon,” Candace answers.

Sage, unfamiliar with wines, answers, “I’ll have one too.”

The waiter drops off two menus and says, “I'll be back with your drinks.” He quickly walks away.

She picks up the menu and starts checking it out, "You looking good tonight." He compliments her.

"Thank you. You are looking kinda hot yourself." She puts her menu down and looks at him, "Tell me about yourself. How long have you been singing?"

He folds his hands and places them on the menu, "Since I was ten, my father, the Reverend, pushed me into singing in the choir."

"Why do you keep calling your father 'the Reverend?'

"I don't know, he made me call him that when I was growing up as a show of respect, and it stuck."

The waiter returns with their cabernet sauvignon and places a glass before each of them.

"Are we ready to order?" He cheerfully inquires.

"Chicken Parmigiana with the house salad and vinaigrette dressing." She replies

Sage quickly picks up the menu. He doesn't know much about Italian food. He sees a picture of spaghetti on the menu, figures it's a safe choice, and closes the menu.

"I'll take the spaghetti with a salad and French dressing." He sips the wine as the waiter picks up the menu from the table.

Candace takes a sip of wine, holds up the glass, looks at the waiter, and proclaims, "Do not let this glass get empty."

The waiter picks up her menu and smiles, “Not a problem, sis.”

He walks away. She takes another sip and places the glass before her, “Tell me more about your family?”

“Well, I am an only child. My parents had me later in life. My dad didn’t want kids until he got his ministry going.”

“Have you ever considered singing as a career?”

He takes a swig of wine, “No, I wasn’t singing because I liked it. The Reverend forced me; I didn’t believe I was good. I don’t know if you saw it, but I get nervous singing in front of people.”

“I noticed it, but we can get past that with the right music and push. The big question is, do you want to sing?”

He shrugs his shoulders and sighs, “Well, to be honest, part of me singing is for fire insurance.”

“Fire insurance? What are you talking about?”

“Hell, fire, brimstone, Satan. Hopefully, my singing in the choir will help balance out some other things about me. I may be a preacher's kid, but I’m no angel.”

Put off by his comments, she takes a big gulp of wine, “You’re not a believer?”

He takes a sip of wine and quietly replies, “I do... but not as strongly as my people do."

The waiter comes back with their orders. He puts down Sage's plate first, then Candace's. He sees she is almost empty. "I will be right back to fill your glass."

Sage pulls his salad in front and pours the dressing on. "Tell me what you think?"

She is also eating her salad, "I see you have the talent. It's raw and needs polishing, but the potential is there. With the right breaks, who knows?"

As she talks, he feels her vibe. He never gave too much thought to singing outside the church.

He smiles at her, a little embarrassed about the comments but mesmerized by her look, and thinks, *Damn, she's a smoke show.* "I don't see a ring. Are you seeing anybody?"

The waiter comes back and fills Candace's glass. Looking at Sage, "Can I top you off, Sir?"

"Go for it, my man." He quickly pours the wine and quietly exits.

Sage takes a drink and repeats the question, "You seeing anyone?"

Taking a bite of her chicken parmigiana, "Let's just stick to music right now."

"So, you're saying there's a chance?"

She laughs heartily but doesn't answer him.

He turns back serious, "You got my interest. What's the next move?"

"Social media. We use it to get your name out there, TikToks, Instagram, Twitter, and anything to get you viral. Go to local talent shows, other churches, anything to get your name out. When the buzz gets big enough, we go to the studio and record a demo."

He slowly shakes his head approvingly, "I like what I'm hearing. I guess this makes us business partners."

Her mouth is full of food. She quickly swallows it and wipes her hands. "Let's make it happen." She offers her hand to make it official.

He wipes his hand, and they shake. "I will have a contract typed up in the next few weeks."

SEVEN

It's late in the afternoon as the sun begins to set. Amira comes to the trap house and parks her white Ford Escape. When she gets out and struts around the back of her vehicle, the four-bangers on the corner check her out.

She stops mid-stride, "What you niggas looking at?" They quickly look away and resume talking.

When she enters the house, she calls, "Q! You here?"

He comes from the bedroom with a six-foot-long black desert cobra snake named Casper draped around his neck. He called it that for the irony of a black snake named after a ghost.

Smiling, he answers, "I was feeding Casper. What's up?"

She screams loudly, quickly jumps back, and presses her back firmly against the door, panic in her voice as she yells, "Get that fucking thing away from me!"

Reveling in her fear, he calmly answers, "Chill the hell out. Your yelling might startle him, and neither of us wants that."

She stares at the snake and quietly states, "I can't talk as long as that thing is in the room." Her hand is still firmly on the doorknob, slowly turning it.

He walks back into his room to put the snake up.

Amira remains at the door, on edge. She doesn't feel comfortable until the snake is locked up.

Q comes back to the living room, his arms spread out like he has nothing to hide, "Casper's in the cage." He walks to Amira and grabs her right hand off the knob. He leads her toward the bedroom. She quickly jerks away, "I didn't come here for that. I need to tell you something."

She stops at the drug table.

"Ok, spit it out." He gruffly answers as he sits down.

Amira takes a seat to the left of him, a little nervous. She looks up at him and blurts out, "Kong is a snitch."

Q jumps out of the chair, sending it crashing to the floor.

"Snitch? That's my dawg. He would never snitch. How you know?" He shakes his head aggressively, refusing to believe it.

Looking up at him calmly, Amira answers, "Well, I'm friendly with this cop who told me."

He walks to the front door, looks at the bangers on the corner, "I don't believe it. That's my boy, we go too far back."

She stands up, walks beside him, and grabs his hand, "I can prove it. The cop told me they were supposed to meet tonight."

He looks at her and angrily questions, "Where?"

"I don't know. He wouldn't tell me. I know they are meeting at midnight."

Q's still looking at the street soldiers, "I'ma come through and get you at ten. Then we're going to Kong's and see what's up. This better be on the up and up."

She protests, "I can't. I don't have nobody to watch my son Aiden. Can't you go by yourself?"

He looks at her disgustedly and retorts as he snatches his hand away from her, "Hoe, you might be setting me up. If anything goes down, you're right there."

She looks at him with equal disdain, "Whatever, fool. Don't hate me; I'm just the messenger."

<<<<>>>>

Amira is sitting on her brown polyester couch, watching her favorite movie, *Sparkle,* in the dark living room. Aiden is asleep, resting on her lap as she rubs his scalp. Her roommate, Ciara, is sitting on a different couch on the other side. Her boyfriend, Shady, sits on the floor between her legs as she braids his hair. Amira's phone buzzes next to her. Outside, there is a horn blowing. They all ignore it while watching the movie.

Amira gets up, leans over, and peeks out the window. She turns her phone over and sees a text from Q: "Let's go. *I'm out here.* Q's in his shiny black SUV, looking at his phone.

She looks away from the window, "Damn, what time is it?"

"Why? What's up?" Ciarra inquires.

She looks at her phone, it's nine forty-five. "Damn, I forgot. Can you watch Aiden? I gotta step out for a couple of hours."

She picks up Aiden, carries him to the bed in her room, and covers him up. She puts on her jeans and sliders. She kisses him on the forehead and turns out the light.

Amira, nervously, says, "Q is waiting downstairs, and you know he doesn't like to be kept waiting."

"What time are you coming back? I got to work in the morning." Ciarra asks.

She walks to the door, "I should be back in a few hours."

Shady looks at Amira, "Yo tell Q I' will get with him tomorrow."

She nods as she opens the door.

Q is still on his phone when she gets in. He puts the phone on the holder, starts the SUV, and gruffly asks, "What took you so long?"

"Relax, fool. I had to put my son to sleep."

He takes off and drives around the block to the next complex. Kong's truck is parked right in front of his door. Q goes past it and backs into a spot to watch.

Unexpectedly, Kong quickly comes out of his apartment and shuffles to his truck.

"Damn, he looks like he is in a hurry. Lucky, we got here when we did." She states.

Q starts up his vehicle, "No thanks to you." He replies snidely.

They are driving through the hood. "Where is this meeting?"

"I told you earlier I don't know."

While driving, Q is careful to stay two to three cars back. "Who is this cop friend who told you this? "

"It's best if you don't know too much. The less you know, the better."

They turn onto the highway, still two car lengths behind. "What? "Bro, you don't trust me?"

She chuckles, "Come on, fool, you see what we're doing. You don't trust me, that's why we're here. I only trust half of what I see and nothing I hear. You ain't new to this."

"I'm going to find out who he is before the night is over." He sneers.

Another ten miles down the road, there is a highway sign advertising Waffle Hut two miles away. Kong exits off the freeway. Q makes sure to slow down so he doesn't get too close as they drive off the ramp. At the end of the road, they veer to the right, and the Waffle Hut is on the left. It is next to a liquor store. Kong turns into the Waffle Hut lot. Q pulls into the liquor store. He pulls up to a fence, and they watch as Kong parks in front and goes inside. Q drives over to the Waffle Hut. He goes further down from where Kong is parked. He backs into a parking spot.

Kong sits down at a booth beside a window. Across from him is a much older, heavier black man. Detective Wally Porter has the same complexion as Kong. His hair is thinning, and his front hairline is receding. His beard is scraggly. He is eating a burger and fries.

They have a clear view of Kong and Porter sitting at the table.

"Is that your boy?" Q asks. She answers, "Yeah, that's him."

Q pulls his phone off the windshield holder and starts recording them.

"Why are you recording? You can't hear what they're saying."

He continues recording without looking at her, "That don't matter; this is a video receipt."

She looks at him as he continues recording.

Kong, sitting at the booth, looks around nervously, leans in, and whispers, "Porter, I can't be seen with you; the wrong fool spots me, and I'm done."

Porter chuckles to himself and takes a big bite of the burger. He looks over Kong's shoulders. With a mouth full, he answers, "Nigga we're twenty-something miles away in this garbage place. It's the middle of the night, ain't nobody thinking about you! Now what you got for me?"

The waitress comes to the table with some silverware and a glass of water and places them in front of Kong.

In a cheerful voice, "What can I get you, hon?"

He looks up at her, smiles, and answers, "Nothing, I'm good."

She smiles back at him and quickly walks away.

He takes a sip of the water. "Later this week, I'm making a pickup in New Elk City."

Munching on some fries, Porter queries, "What time? What day? Give me something."

"Look, man, I told you all I know. Q talks only when necessary. When I find out more, I will get with you."

Porter drinks his tea, "You wouldn't be holding out on me, would you?"

Kong insulted by the insinuation, "Porter, I've been upfront ever since we had this arrangement."

The detective stares at him and lets out a small "Humph." He slides a cell phone to him, "Here, take this."

"What's this?" Kong asks as he takes a sip of water.

"It's a burner. I meant to get it to you at our last meeting. Use it to contact me. I don't want you pissing yourself the next time we get together."

Kong grabs the phone and places it in his gray hoodie.

Porter takes another bite of the burger, "Thanks for nothing. Please don't hit me up unless you got something. I've got better things to do than waste time with lowlifes like you." He finishes the burger and gulps the tea. Kong stares at him with mild disgust as he gobbles down the burger. Porter, irritated, blurts out, "Why are you still here?"

Kong chuckles at his disrespectful attitude. He stands up, "I don't know how long I will be doing this. I sent my highlights to a few colleges and got a recruiter interested. Hopefully, I can get a scholarship."

In a sarcastic tone, Porter replies, "That's great. It's so good to hear that you trying to improve your life. I hope you stick to our agreement. It would be unfortunate to lose your chance because your record gets out."

He slowly shakes his head, "Bro, why are you such an asshole? I will stick to our agreement. You do know extortion is a felony?" He turns and walks away.

Porter stands up and yells, "Are you threatening me? I can arrest you before you reach that door. You do what you need to, and we won't have any problems." Kong continues walking and leaves.

Q and Amira see him leave and quickly duck. They stay down until they hear him go. They sit back up and see Porter talking with the waitress, paying for his meal.

Q "I've got what I need." In a confident tone, Amira states, "I guess you believe me now. What you going to do about it?"

"Don't worry about it. I will take care of it."

"What do you think they were talking about?" Amira questions, pressing him.

He hears the question and is perplexed. He is pissed that his boy is talking to a cop in the middle of the night. He knows he has to do something. If he doesn't do something, the respect he gained is lost.

Q unexpectedly opens the door, Amira grabs his right bicep as he exits the vehicle and yells, "Where you going?"

He angrily snatches his arm away from her and, with his right hand, palms her head and pushes it away from him. In a menacing tone tells her, "Trick, don't you ever be putting your hands on me! Never! I need to talk to your man."

He slams the door and walks to the restaurant.

EIGHT

Kong's relaxing in the green recliner, playing a video game. He checks the time, it's 1245 in the morning. The message *makes the pickup appear* at the top of his screen in the middle of the game.

He exhales deeply and replies, "On it." He releases the recliner, stands up, and slowly walks to the bedroom down the hall. Brigette is asleep and lightly snoring. Carefully, he sits on the edge of the bed to avoid waking her. She shifts position as she senses his weight on the mattress.

In a sleepy hoarse voice, she inquires, "You going somewhere?"

"I got that run to New Elk City for a pick-up."

"What pick-up? What time is it?" She rolls over and turns on the nightstand lamp.

"You didn't need to turn on the lights. I didn't want to wake you." He gets up, steps into the closet, and puts on his jeans

On the nightstand is her phone. "It's almost one. Why you leaving so late to go to New Elk?"

He's looking for his shoes under the bed and answers, "No traffic, no po-po, get down the road, make the pickup, and I'm back home."

Leaning toward him sternly, and demands, "You still haven't told him you're getting out of the game?"

Kong doesn't reply as he ties his kicks, then stands up and faces her, saying, "I promise after I make this run, I'll give him the heads up."

"I've heard that before. You need to decide whether it's me and your son or this life. You know I'm your ride-or-die, but not for this."

Kong goes in for a quick kiss. They nearly touch their nose, and he whispers to her, "I can't believe you're questioning where my heart is. Next week I'm going to State to meet with the coaches. Then I'll get that scholarship, get back into football, and start a new life."

She corrects him as he gets up, "WE will start a new life."

Chuckling, he answers, "Yeah, that's what I meant. Catch you in the morning. He grabs his keys and phone from the dresser. She turns off the light.

He decides to take her blue minivan. Before he starts it, he texts Big Saint, *OMW, to New Elk for a pickup. You wanna roll?*

He already knows the answer as he is driving to Big Saint's house.

At a stoplight. The phone pings; it's a text from Big Saint. Yeah, *homey, you on the way?*

He texts back, "*I'll be there in 10 minutes*." *Be outside.*

Kong comes to a stoplight and picks up the burner phone off the passenger seat.

He stares at it, like it's poison ivy, contemplating if he should make the call.

The light turns green, and he is oblivious to the car behind him. The horn blowing brings him back to the moment. He drops the phone in the passenger seat and accelerates away from the light.

Kong quickly turns right into an all-night gas station and picks up the phone. He looks at it like

Detective Porter, it's the one number stored on it. The phone rings five times a gruff voice answers, "You calling at this time? It better be good."

"I'm just sticking to our agreement."

"C'mon, man, what you got?"

"On my way to make the pick-up in New Elk."

This gets Porter's attention, and he sits up in the bed, "What's the pickup? How much weight?"

"Don't know."

"Where's the drop off at?"

"The trap at 187."

"Aight." Porter hangs up.

Surprised by the quick hang-up, Kong looks at the phone and puts it in the glove box. He finishes the drive to Big Saint's house.

Saint is sitting on the trunk of his car, drifting off as Kong pulls in behind him. He jumps off the trunk and shuffles over.

"What's up, Cuz?"

"Appreciate you making this run, Saint."

Big Saint gets in and quickly adjusts his seat to get comfortable, pressing it against Luke's car seat, which prevents it from reclining further.

"Damn, Kong, big as you are, why are you riding around in this toy truck?"

Kong chuckles, "Bro, this gets us around. That's the only thing that matters."

Sage lies back in the seat and yawns, "I guess I'm not getting any sleep tonight. Tomorrow is going to be a long day." He turns away towards the passenger door. He looks out the window and sees a pimp push a prostitute onto the ground and kick her in the stomach. He yells at her while she is on the ground. Watching this pisses him off. The Rev taught him never to raise his hand to a woman. He clenches his right hand into a fist to control his anger.

"Yo bro, put your seatbelt on," Kong instructs him.

Ignoring Kong's comment, he states, “I hate seeing a man beating on women,”

“What are you talking about?”

He closes his eyes, “Nothing, forget about it. I'm going to sleep.”

“You do you. Tonight's my last run; I'm out.”

Saint hears this and turns around, “No shit, this it?”

As they drive down the empty roads to the expressway, Kong answers, “Jet put it down, it's either her and Luke or this.”

“That's just the push you need. You really care about her, huh?”

“Yeah, dogg, we have been together on and off since the eighth grade. I believe she's the one.”

“She is the one… the only one you've ever been with,” Sage jokes.

Kong lets out a small chuckle. “Yeah, whatever, fool. After I get this scholarship, we will move, get a place together, and start a new life. With some luck, I could go pro.”

“I hear you, boy! Making big moves and doing things,” he responds excitedly. “I got something cooking myself. That date I had with Candace, that music producer was fire.”

“Aight, I hear you.”

“She's fine as hell, cuz. I'm trying to get with her.”

Laughing, Kong answers, “What’s up with your singing?”

“She's down for that, too. We're meeting soon to talk more about it.” Big Saint lies back down in the seat and turns to the door. “Now, can you shut the hell up so I can sleep?”

“Aight, cuz, say less, I need to hit up Q for the address.”

At the stoplight, Kong waits to turn on the expressway. He reaches for the phone and texts, *On the expressway, what’s the address?*

The light turns green, he makes the right onto the ramp. Big Saint is knocked out, snoring in the passenger’s seat.

Kong settles in, knowing he has a two-hour drive ahead. He turns on the radio and listens to some old-school hip-hop.

He wonders why Q hasn’t answered his text and whether he should call. He passes a road sign reading "New Elk City 95 miles."

Reading the sign, he sees he still has some time.

Q texts back, *1113 Camden Blvd, New Elk City.*

As he continues down the dark highway with Saint snoring, he pulls up the phone's GPS.

While entering the address, another text comes in. *Get back with me when you thirty minutes out.*

He texts back *Bet.*

He punches the address into the GPS. It shows it to be about two hours and 20 minutes away. He looks at the minivan's clock; it's 2:30 am.

Kong thinks *we probably won't get there before three. Then factor in about 30 minutes for the pickup, and we'll be lucky if we make it home by six.*

Q's at the trap house at the table with a mason jar of buds and the scale. Shady, asleep, stretched out on the couch, his marine brother is the enforcer with the 187's

As Q seals a baggy, his phone on the table beside the jar buzzes with a text from Porter: *Your boy Kong checked in on the way to New Elk. Everything still on?"*

He picks up the phone and texts, *Mission still on. Shady will meet you at the Bally Apts. I'll* get *back to you.*

Kong places the phone back on the table. It pings again with another text, *Don't fuck me over, you won't live long enough to regret it.*

Q glances at the text, chuckles, and mumbles in a low, menacing voice, "This dirty 5-0 here… threatening me."

He gets up, walks over to Shady, and kicks his feet as they lie on the edge of the couch. "SHADY! SHADY! Get up! I got a job for you. We need to talk about a few things before you make this run."

He sleepily sits up on the couch and rubs his eyes angrily, “What Nigga! Damn, can’t get any sleep at home, can’t get any sleep here! What the fuck, bro!”

“Chill, get your shit together. Sleep when you're dead.”

Q returns to the table, grabs the bong, and hands it too Shady.

He fires it up, takes a long toke, holds it for a few seconds, and slowly releases it.

Shady sits back on the couch and places the bong on the coffee table. He looks up at Q, “What’s the mission?”

Q, sitting beside him on the couch, tells him, “That situation we discussed earlier. I need you to take care of it tonight.”

<<<<>>>>

Big Saint earlier complained about not getting any sleep in the passenger seat is actually knocked out, sawing logs. Kong is speeding along the four-lane expressway. He shoots past an expressway sign that reads "New Elk City 30 miles."

He calls Q, and he answers after the first ring.

“Thirty minutes away?”

His quick response surprises Kong, “Just pass the 30 miles out sign. Yo, what exactly am I doing?”

"I need to hit them up to let them know you're close. Go to the GPS spot. Don't blow the horn or do anything. They will approach you and drop off the packages. You run it back here. Everything's been taken care of."

"Say no more, I got it." Kong answers.

"You, my boy, I trust you don't let me down."

"It's all good." Kong hangs up.

Big Saint remains asleep, facing the passenger window. Kong punches him on the left shoulder and shouts, "Yo, Saint, wake up, fool, we're almost there." Kong stays alert, aware that unpredictable things can happen in moments like this. Expect the unexpected.

Saint groggily rolls over to face him, "What's up?"

"We're half an hour away. You need to be woke and on point when we roll up."

He puts the car seat upright, "Alright, cuz I'm good."

Big Saint stretches to further awaken himself.

"When we're done, I'm crashing again."

"Whatever. I need you to be ready if anything happens." Big Saint opens the center console, and the 9mm sits on the ready.

"After we make the pickup, we get some gas and head back home."

Kong looks at the GPS; it reads twenty-five miles away and 18 minutes to the destination.

Big Saint snaps, “It’s about to go down in eighteen minutes." He glares at the GPS. "The factory district seems about right.” Kong quickly texts: Q *We are 18 minutes out.*

The text is promptly answered with, *"I’ll give them the heads-up."*

They exit the expressway. Big Saint glances at Kong nervously and says, “Bro, I have a bad feeling about this.”

“Yeah, me too.”

NINE

The GPS guides them to an old, abandoned building in the warehouse district. It's located on the corner. The five-story, faded-brown brick building has broken windows scattered across its floors. It's 3:15 in the morning, with no traffic on the street. The building is on the left side of the road, and Kong U-turns to park directly in front of it.

"This is the spot I don't see anybody," Kong states as he looks around at the empty streets.

Big Saint flips up the center console and grabs the piece. He pulls back the slide to see if it's loaded. "Stay alert."

Kong calls Q, *"What the hell is going on? We here and don't see nobody. This feels sketchy."*

"*Niggas relax. I just spoke with them they on the way. Ten minutes tops. Park in the front loading zone. Flash your light so they know it's you."*

Kong's confused by the order, *"What front-loading zone spot?"*

Big Saint looks behind them and sees three parking spots underneath the building. He answers, "It's behind us."

Kong looks back and sees the opening, "Aight Q, ten minutes we out. With or without the dope." He hangs up.

"Back up and park. We can see them coming and get out quickly if needed."

Kong begins by starting the car, nodding decisively. He quickly reverses into the central parking spot, with the engine roaring. The loud noise of distant motorcycle engines cuts through the night air. After parking, he turns off the lights, blanketing the scene in darkness.

He looks at Big Saint, "Ten minutes, bro. We out, Cool?"

"Cool."

The motorcycles become louder. They are approaching swiftly and aggressively, "Are they riding bikes?" Kong inquires.

Big Saint, with a confused expression, shrugs his shoulders.

Two crotch rockets shoot before them. Kong quickly flashes his lights as they turn into the building and park on the left side of the vehicle. They are in all-black riding gear, wearing full-face helmets. One of them is wearing a black backpack. The one without the pack walks in front, coming towards them.

Big Saint grabs the gun out of his lap and places it in his right hand, and puts it on the side by the door.

The only light in the area comes from the street lamp, and they see only the riders' silhouettes.

The rider in front stops at Kong's window and taps it with his gloved right hand. He yells through the helmet, "Pop the trunk."

Kong reaches down the door panel, pushes the button, and hears the click. The second rider walks around and goes to the back of the minivan. He removes his backpack, opens the hatch, and places it in the vehicle. Both riders walk to their bikes and take off.

Kong starts up the car, "Damn, that was easy."

"We need to check out the product to ensure everything is legit." Big Saint states.

Kong pulls out of the loading zone and parks under the streetlight, saying, "Go look" to Big Saint.

Big Saint gets out and shuffles to the hatch as Kong pops it. He grabs the backpack and unzips it. There are ten sealed bags of weed in the pack. He opens one of the bags, takes a whiff, and the familiar scent is there.

"We straight." He gathers the bags together and puts them back in the pack. Big Saint puts the pack on his shoulder and shuts the hatch.

He opens the door, puts the bag in the back seat, and enters the vehicle.

Big Saint grunts, "Let's go."

TEN

Kong's droopy-eyed and barely awake. He exits off the expressway and stops at the traffic light. He lets down the window to get some fresh air to help him stay awake. Big Saint is once again knocked out in the passenger seat. They are back home on the way to the trap. Kong's light turns green, and he lazily accelerates through the intersection. On the other side of the intersection is a single dark blue sedan. The sedan explodes from the light, Kong anxiously turns to his right. He is petrified with fear as the sedan barrels towards them and crashes into Big Saint's door. Kong's vehicle careens off the roadside, veering wildly before crashing into a nearby light pole with a thunderous impact. The sedan screeches to a stop in the middle of the intersection.

Big Saint was not wearing his seatbelt, and his body was thrown over into Kong. This causes Kong's head to slam into the driver's door window. The left side of his head is bleeding heavily after hitting the glass, with blood streaming down his cheek. He pushes Big Saint off of him and yells, "Saint! Saint" as he shakes his limp body. He doesn't get an answer, not knowing if he is dead or alive. Through the deflating airbags, two masked men in all black get out of the car about 30 yards away and make their way to him. The driver motions with his right hand for the other guy to spread out to take the rear of the vehicle. They creep tactically toward the car. Kong frantically tries to open his door, but it is jammed shut because of the light pole. He desperately looks at the men swiftly approaching. They are now twenty yards away, still carefully creeping toward them. He unbuckles his seat belt, reaches down, and presses the button for the back hatch release. Opening the center console and grabs the piece and climbs into the back seat. His head is throbbing intensely with a relentless pounding, blood seeping from the wound. His neck is cruelly stiffening, each movement increasingly painful. Kong is a dead man if he stays in the car; his heart is thumping with fear. He's taking quick, shallow breaths to control his nerves; his whole body is trembling uncontrollably. *I can't go out like no punk*, he thinks to himself. Seeing the weed on the floor of the back seat. He thinks about grabbing it, but decides against it because it will slow him down. One of the men is about ten yards away. Kong knows he has to get out before he gets any closer. He takes three deep breaths to psyche himself up. Tightly clenching the gun, he pushes the back hatch open and barrel rolls out. The gunman sees this and fires two quick shots, both missing high and smashing the back glass with a loud crash. Kong rapidly fires two fierce shots in retaliation as he dashes behind the vehicle to escape. The gunman ducks swiftly and quickly retreat's back toward his sedan.

The sedan starts up. Kong is crouched behind the rear tire and holds the gun with both hands; the barrel is at the tip of his nose. Frantically, he moves his head right and left, searching for the shooters. Terrified, he thinks, *they're gonna ram us again. I can't give him a chance. I need to take him out.* The vehicle is racing towards him without thinking, and he quickly stands up and starts firing shots. The second gunman, crouched near the front passenger tire of Kong's vehicle, suddenly rises, catching him off guard, and fires one shot that strikes him in the dead center of his forehead. The gun drops out of his hand as he crumples to the ground with blood trickling from the bullet hole.

The driver of the sedan quickly stops about five yards from the SUV. He jumps out and stands at the door and yells to the other gunman, "Yo check, make sure he's done."

The shooter points his pistol and yells back to the driver, "Don't give me orders." He walks around the front of the vehicle.

"Check yourself, fool," the driver yells back at him. The shooter walks around the front of Kong's vehicle, looks inside, and sees Big Saint's body slumped in the front seat. He opens the rear door and shoots one round into the top of Big Saint's head.

"What the hell, bro?" The driver yells. "Finishing the job, if I'm doing a job, I'm doing it right." He retorts.

"You sure you a cop? You straight ruthless."

Detective Porter, the shooter, walks over and kicks Kong's lifeless body. He notices a single bullet hole in Kong's forehead, the blood flow slowing down.

Porter walks over to the back passenger door, opens it, and grabs the backpack. They both get back in the sedan.

As Shady starts up the sedan, "Now, let's finish the deal," Porter tells Shady.

The Metamorphosis

Therefore, if anyone is in Christ, the creation has come: The old has gone, the new is here

2 Corinthians 5:17

ELEVEN

Sage's eyes snap open as he notices a ceiling fan spinning overhead. He finds himself in his room, lying in bed. Although the fan is running, he cannot hear or feel its breeze. The house is eerily silent—no sounds, no smells, nothing. Confused about what's happening, he tries to get up but remains frozen in bed. He attempts to lift his right arm, but nothing moves; the same occurs with his left. He then tries to raise his head to look at his legs, but he's unable to move. Eventually, he tries to move his legs — first the right, then the left — but his entire body is paralyzed. The only thing he can move are his eyes, which frantically scan the room. Panic sets in completely.

"MOM! DAD!" He tries to yell. No sounds come out of his mouth.

A beam of light shines down from the ceiling to the left of the fan. From this glow, his mother appears, her figure softly shimmering. She floats effortlessly about three feet above him, as he lies motionless on the bed. Wearing a pure white flowing robe that seems to ripple with an unseen breeze, she emits a gentle, ethereal light.

"Relax, son, everything will be fine." She speaks in a calm, soothing voice.

“What’s going on? Am I dead? Where’s Dad?” He asked in a frantic tone.

He is talking but making no sound, yet she can hear him. They are communicating telepathically.

“All the answers will come in time. You are not dead. What is the last thing you remember?”

“I was in the car with Kong returning from picking up... a package. I fell asleep on the way home. I don’t remember anything after that.”

Smiling at him, she glides closer and lightly touches the back of his left hand. Her touch lifts him out of bed. They enter a tube filled with a bright light, are whisked away, and instantly appear in a hospital room.

He is currently in the Intensive Care Unit (ICU), unconscious on an elevated hospital bed. A white bandage is applied around his head. Multiple medical devices are connected to him, including a ventilator, an electrocardiogram (EKG), a wound vacuum, and Sequential Compression Devices (SCDs) on his legs.

He looks down at himself, in an unconscious condition, shocked. “Am I dying? How long have I been like that?”

Before she can answer, his father and Candace come into the room. They walk over to his bed. Candace rubs her fingers on his hand as the EKG beeps in the background. Stephon is standing beside her, and they look down at him.

She looks at the Reverend, "Thank you for allowing me to visit Sage."

He looks away from Sage and softly states, "I know we never got a chance to meet, but to hear him talk about you and see his excitement, I knew he liked you."

She smiles at him, "I saw it too. I was trying to keep it professional between us." Pausing, she looks down at him with the EKG beeping, and her eyes are misting up, "Is he going to die?"

The door opens, and Sydney and a nurse enter the room.

Sage's entity floats overhead and looks at Sydney. "What are you?"

She calmly tells him, "In time, everything will be explained." They hover above as the nurse approaches the other side of the bed. She takes out a small flashlight, leans over him, opens his eye, and shines the light to check pupil reaction. There is no response.

All three are watching anxiously. The nurse grimly turns off the light, then checks the EKG and walks around the bed.

"No change," she pauses before them, "I'll return in an hour to feed him."

"How do you feed him?" Candace asks.

"Through the tube in his nose. I got other patients I need to check on." She quickly walks out.

Sydney walks over to the other side of the bed where the nurse was.

Standing over him, she gazes at him in bed and gently says, “Everything will be alright, son." She takes his hand and gives it a gentle squeeze. “We just finished our service. Your friend Candace visited you today," then looks up at her and smiles.

Still smiling, she looks back down at him and continues, “Aiden is fine. I haven’t brought him to see you yet. I don’t believe seeing you like this would be good for him.”

As Sydney continues speaking to Sage, Candace questions Stephon, “How did this happen?”

“From what the police told us, Sage and his friend Kong were driving when another car deliberately crashed into them. His friend Kong was shot in the head and killed. Sage was shot in the head but somehow didn’t die. The bullet grazed his front lobe, causing bruising, torn tissues, and bleeding. The doctor says he is lucky to be alive between the crash and the gunshot. I’m not too fond of the word luck. I say he is favored. ‘*So, do not fear for I am with you; do not be dismayed, for I am your God. I will strengthen you and help you; I will uphold you with my righteous right hand.”*

Sydney, hearing the scripture, shakes her head in agreement, “Isaiah 41:10.”

Both entities are looking down, and without warning, she gently touches his hand, causing them both to fade into a white light. They reappear, floating above a snowy, jagged mountain range at night. The sky is a stunning swirl of white, blue, and pink lights that illuminates the night sky. Sage has never seen anything like it. He is awestruck by the sight. As they float above the mountains, Sydney's entity says, "We can talk now."

TWELVE

Sage feels a rush of emotions and doesn't know where to begin.

The spiritual entity senses his emotional state and communicates, "I am your earthly mother but also what you consider an angel."

He is captivated by all that unfolds around him. Above the mountains, a starry ribbon of light twinkles in the background. Her form suddenly shifts into that of an eight-foot-tall black woman, dressed in a flowing white robe that drapes from her head to her feet. Majestic, glowing white wings, four feet long, extend from her back. A gold halo appears above her head, casting a golden light that envelops her entire body.

"I am what you think I am, a protector angel. Some call us guardian angels. We are called several names by different religions."

"Are you the reason I'm still alive?" He asks.

"No. I did not interfere. I cannot stop what is destined to happen. You survived because it was not your time. The Creator grants humans free will to choose their paths. From birth, all beings are accompanied by moral and immoral angels that constantly influence their decisions.

The more you follow a certain path, the stronger these angels become and guide your life, while the others weaken but never leave. They remain nearby, ready to re-emerge. Just one moment or choice can shift your compass in the opposing direction."

Sage listens to all this but does not understand how it relates to him. "What's this got to do with me?"

She continues, "The wrong protectors have guided you. This experience has given you a chance to start anew. As I said, all it takes is one opportunity for the weaker to become stronger. This is that opportunity."

"We belong to an ancient secret society known as Equipoise, whose mission is to maintain balance across the universe. It oversees cosmic stability and intervenes when necessary. Throughout history, select individuals have been granted special gifts to augment their physical and spiritual qualities. Your earthly mother was given this opportunity. Now, you have the chance to receive these gifts as well, should you choose to accept the challenge."

Sage, even more confused than ever, "My mom is an angel?"

"Not an 'emissary,' your mother had the opportunity to receive the gifts. She declined because she met your father and fell in love. She chose family over the gifts, feeling she wasn't ready to take on the responsibilities that come with them."

"Gifts! What are these gifts?" He emotes with frustration.

"The gifts are your body and spirit, which will be magnified beyond those of a normal person. You will be stronger, faster, and have increased mental abilities. You will be superior to other people."

Sage, hearing this, inquires, "You mean like a superhero?"

"Superhero?" She continues not reacting to the comment. "You will be challenged and placed in a different, unfamiliar life. You will have no memory of your present situation. The new life you partake in be will be natural to you."

Sage is wary; he doesn't know what circumstances he will be stepping into or how long it will take. Is this situation a life-and-death ordeal? He asks, "Could I die?"

"I have told you everything I'm allowed to say." She answers.

"What happens to me if I don't accept it?"

"You will be sent back to your body. I have no control over what happens after that. You need to decide."

The being hovering in the night sky slowly waves her right hand over the starry horizon. A bright light flashes about two hundred yards away. Two gigantic, fifty-foot-arched wooden castle doors appear. The one on the right is black, with a faint flicker beneath it; the other door is glowing white.

“The light door is the path to redemption, absolution. The other leads back to the life from whence you came.”

Sage looks at the towering doors. He contemplates: "*Am I worthy of all this? My mom is a better person than me and didn’t want this.*"

“You need to choose, or it will be chosen for you.”

“I’ve made my choice.” He glides towards his chosen door

THIRTEEN

Stephon and Sydney are alone in the elevator after visiting Sage. They are both silent, lost in their thoughts. Both are experiencing the heaviness of the moment, as if they are carrying a backpack full of rocks. Sage has been in the hospital for over a month, and there has not been any improvement. They will get something to eat and return later in the afternoon. The elevator arrives at the bottom floor and opens. As they leave and turn left, walking to the exits about fifty yards away, Amira, Q, and Aiden enter the hospital. The lobby is full of doctors, nurses, and medical staff scurrying in the hall. Both sides are oblivious as they walk toward each other about fifty yards away. Aiden sees Sydney. He yells out, "Maw maw," and quickly takes off. Amira, hearing this, looks ahead and sees Stephon and Sydney. Aiden weaves through the crowded hallway like he is on a football field. She sees him running to her and squats down to greet him, and he runs into her arms.

"Hey, Maw maw." He yells during the hug. "Did you see my dad?"

Trying to sound cheerful, she answers, "I sure did."

Amira and Q approach, Sydney stands up, and Aiden walks back and stands beside his mom.

"How's he doing?" Amira asks Sydney. In a somber tone, she answers, "The same, no change." With a worried look, she asks, "Do you think it's good for Aiden to see him like this?"

Amira, offended by the question, states, "He misses his father, and I don't believe in hiding anything from my son. He needs to see the bad and good in the world."

"That's fine, I just don't want my grandson traumatized seeing his father half dead."

"He's your grandson. My son. Know your place." Amira brazenly tells her.

Matching her energy, Sydney snaps and steps forward. "My place?' Is doing what I need to do to look out for my grandson. Do we need to step outside?"

"Come on now. We don't need to take it there." Stephon offers as he pulls Sydney back.

Q sees the scene's awkwardness and offers his hand to Stephon, "What's up? I'm Quinton. I go by 'Q.'

The Reverend recognizes 'Q' from hearing Sage talk, looks down at his hand with disdain, and does not attempt to shake it. He indignantly replies, "You in that gang with my son."

Q arrogantly corrects him, "I am the O.G. of the 187."

"You're the reason my son's in this place!" Stephon angrily retorts.

“You old fool, you don’t know what you're talking about. Big Saint being down ain’t on me. You'd best stop talking crazy to me.”

Stephon is not backing down, “Son ain’t nobody afraid of you. The only thing I fear is God. Despite what you believe, you ain’t him. ‘Show proper respect to everyone, love the family…

Q dismissively waves his hand at Stephon, “Shut up, old man! Don’t nobody care about no damn bible!”

Stephon, heated, steps towards Q and points his right index finger in Q’s face, “Don’t ever disrespect the Bible in my presence.”

Now Sydney grabs Stephon’s shoulders from behind to pull him away, “Look at you, you're trying to control me, and now you're losing it. Let’s go, Step. We don’t need to be getting kicked out of here.”

He lets himself be pulled away as he walks backward to the automatic doors. Q yells at him, “Another time, another place, you gonna learn some respect.”

“Step, he doesn’t matter. God and family are the only things we need to be worried about.” Sydney whispers to him as they hold hands and leave the hospital.

FOURTEEN

"You have made your decision. Now you face two different real-life situations you know nothing about. How you handle each one will determine if you are granted your gifts," the celestial creature announces as they float above his body, lying in his hospital room.

"I don't understand what I am supposed to be doing?" He exclaims.

Without answering him, she opens the bright portal, and he is whisked away into it. Stepping into a brand-new life.

Jeb Dumas is a committed Christian and devoted family man. He and his wife, Holly, are the founders and owners of The Dumas Family Barbeque, a highly successful family-run business. He is 65 years old and has been married to Holly for over 40 years; she is his one true love. They have seven children, five boys and two girls. All their children are grown, married, and have kids of their own. They have 12 grandchildren, ranging in age from 3 to 18. The oldest son, Ty, is celebrating his thirty-fifth birthday with the entire family at the restaurant. Jeb and Holly had to leave early because she was feeling unwell. They drive in his gray Lexus SUV to their home in the upscale Candlewood subdivision. The car is quiet, with no radio or conversation, as Holly needs silence to cope with her headache. She has her seat reclined, eyes closed, trying to deal with her pounding head. He turns left into the driveway and circles around the back of their ivory brick split-level home. The garage is located at the rear of the house, and the door is already open.

He hits the touchscreen monitor to shut the door. He gently shakes her left shoulder to awaken her and whispers, “Darling, we're home. Do you feel any better?”

She wakes up holding her forehead with her right hand, “No. It feels like it’s getting worse. The nausea is kicking in.”

He walks around the front of the vehicle, opens the door, and helps her out. She enters the pantry, still holding her head as he closely follows to make sure she doesn’t stumble. They head directly to the kitchen. The house is quiet and dark. He turns on the light switch. The recessed lighting illuminates the ivory cabinets and floors. She trips slightly because of the sudden brightness. She leans on the coffee-colored granite counters. He steadies her by grabbing her shoulders.

She stubbornly yells out, “I’m alright. Please leave me alone! I’m going to lie down.”

He knows when she's in her mood, it’s best to let her be. He lets go of her shoulders. “Okay, babe.” He softly pats her right hand on the counter. She slowly walks to the bedroom.

"I will get you a glass of water to take your pills." She does not respond but shakes her head to acknowledge his comment.

He walks over to the ivory overhead cabinet and grabs a whiskey glass. Then, he heads to the fridge to get ice and water from the outside door. He goes to their bedroom, where she sits up, propped by several throw pillows on their king-size bed. She has a blue migraine head cap wrapped around her head, covering her eyes. Near the bed is the nightstand. He reaches into the top drawer and takes out a pill bottle. Sitting beside her on the bed, he opens the bottle and holds out her left hand, pouring two blue pills into it. She pops the pills into her mouth and then receives a glass of water.

"I'm sorry about snapping at you earlier, but you know these headaches can be so intense that I lash out."

Chuckling, he hugs her and says, "No need to apologize. I know you didn't mean anything by it. We've been together too many years." He lets go and stands up, "I'm going to let you rest and go to the living room and watch the game. Let me know if you need anything."

"Thank you, dear. I'm just going to sit here until I drift off."

Jeb leaves the room, goes back to the kitchen, and grabs another whiskey glass along with a cold can of cola. He walks across the oak hardwood floors into the living room and sits in his black leather massage chair. Above the fireplace on the beige-painted walls, there's a fifty-five-inch LED smart TV. He places the cola on the lamp table to the left, grabs the TV remote, and turns it on. Then he retrieves a bottle of brandy and a cigar from the bottom of the table, pours some into the glass, and pops open the cola. He puts the cigar in the glass and mixes the drink with it. Taking a small sip, he relaxes in the chair and thinks, *Damn, I deserve this.* He quietly watches and sips his brandy.

<<<<>>>>

The ringing front doorbell awakens Jeb. Between the massage chair and the glass of brandy, he dozed off. He is a little buzzed as he gets up out of the chair. Walking to the front door, he sees a police car through the door sidelights. He is anxious; he cannot think of any reason the police would be coming by his house at night. He answers the door, and much to his surprise, there is a fireman and a police officer at the door.

“Is there a problem, officer?” Jeb inquires.

The policeman speaks first, “Good evening. I’m Sgt. Corey Jackson with the Mountain Lake PD, and this is Lt. Marcus Jamison. Are you Jeb Dumas, owner of the Dumas Family Barbeque?”

“Yes, sir. Why? What happened?” He asks nervously.

“Can we come in? We need to speak with you about a situation that occurred tonight.”

He looks at the fireman, who has a grim, distressed look on his face. “Come in.”

FIFTEEN

Jeb's heart pounds with fear as he notices the police and fire crews arriving, signaling trouble. They enter the living room and sit on the golden yellow leather couch to the right of his massage chair, with the policeman on the left and the fireman on the right. A half-hour sitcom rerun plays on the TV. Jeb, sitting in his massage chair, fixates on them and asks somberly, "What's going on?"

Holly walks in from the hallway she hears the commotion. Her migraine cap is pulled up on her head. Seeing the public officials in her house, she panics, "Why are the police here? Is everything alright?"

Jeb stands up and motions for her to come over. She takes a seat on the armrest of the massage chair. He sits back down. "Calm down, honey. They just got here."

Jeb looks at them and asks, "Alright, what's going on?"

They look nervously at each other, unsure who should speak first. The fireman nods to the policeman, signaling him to go ahead. He takes a breath and swallows hard, "I'm so sorry to have to tell you that there was a fire at your restaurant, which was totally destroyed."

"Oh, my God!" Holly screams, her voice trembling with shock and fear. Jeb remains still, eyes locked forward with no response. “No! No!” Holly’s voice echoes as she suddenly drops her head into her hands, her shoulders trembling as she begins to cry uncontrollably.

The policeman continues, “There were people inside, and as of right now, we have not been able to locate any survivors.”

“That was our family! Kids and Grandkids!” She screams at the cop.

She gets up and shuffles quickly out of the room, sobbing uncontrollably.

Both officials are taken aback by her outburst. The fireman quickly responds, “We're sorry, we didn’t know.”

Jeb didn’t hear the apology; his attention was fully absorbed by the television, which was broadcasting coverage of the devastating fire. The images on the screen haunt him. The building’s roof is torn apart, jagged edges exposed to the sky, and thick, black smoke billows from the wreckage. Tiny flames flicker among the rubble, stubbornly refusing to die out. Shaking his head in disbelief, he whispers under his breath, “How?’

It was spoken so softly that they didn’t hear him. The policeman leaned towards him, “Excuse me? Did you ask, How?”

In an angrier, louder tone, he replies, “Yes! How did this happen?”

The fireman speaks up, “We haven’t been able to confirm it yet, but with the explosion's size and the building's damage, we suspect it was a gas leak. Your wife said it was your family there. Do you know how many people were in the building?”

The news has now moved on to a different story. He looks at them with tears welling in his eyes, “We had closed the restaurant early. It was my oldest son Ty’s birthday, and the whole family was there. Holly and I left early because she was coming down with one of her migraines. With all the kids, wives, husbands, and grandkids, it was probably between twenty and twenty-five people. You haven’t found any survivors?”

“Currently, with the few bodies recovered, we have no survivors. The explosion and the size of the fire make the chances of finding anyone else very slim.”

Jeb steadily shakes his head and asks the fireman, “What do you need from me?”

The policeman says, “Umm, I know this is not a good time, but when things have settled down in the next few days, could you help identify some of your family members?”

Those are words he never imagined hearing, even in a thousand years. He lets out a deep sigh and slowly nods.

From the bedroom, Holly is sobbing hysterically.

“If there isn’t anything else, I need to check on my wife.”

All three men stand up, and the fireman speaks, “We understand, sir. We had to inform you personally instead of you hearing it from the media.”

All three men walk towards the door, and the policeman stops and turns to Jeb, “I’m sure I speak for the entire Police Department when I say we are truly sorry for your loss.” The fireman shakes his head in agreement. He then reaches out and hugs Jeb, and the policeman does the same. They leave.

As he walks into the bedroom, Holly is crying uncontrollably, her body trembling with grief. When he reaches her, she is kneeling, clutching the edge of the bed, her head bowed in despair. He slowly kneels beside her, wrapping his right arm gently around her shoulders, and softly whispers, “Are you going to be okay?”

She lifts her head off the bed, her eyes bloodshot from crying, and looks at him with loathing, shouting, “Am I going to be alright! Did you not hear what they said? Our kids and grandkids all died tonight! How the hell can I be okay?”

In a softer, smoother tone, he answers, “I'm at a loss. I don’t know what to say. We need to pray for the strength to endure.”

“Pray?!” Her voice trembles with rage. "Don’t talk to me about praying! We’ve been going to church and praying; I’ve been praying my whole life. Trusting in GOD! You're a deacon and on the board of trustees, and this is our reward? We lost everything in one night. EVERYTHING!! Her voice filled with a mix of grief and anger. What kind of God does that?"

He lashes back at her, "You don't think I'm hurting!? It was my family, too. You can't quit on GOD now!! Everything happens for a reason, even if we don't understand it. We need his strength and guidance more than ever. If we were ever believers, now is the time to show it. Would you please pray with me?"

She slowly shakes her head no, then repeats her earlier question, "What kind of fair and just GOD would take away our entire family in one night?"

He gets off his knees, sits on the bed, and looks at her. "He is the almighty, the Alpha, and the Omega. It is neither my place nor my right to question or try to explain why this happened. All I can say is that if we are willing to accept the material blessings he has given us, we must also accept that there will be suffering. If you don't want to pray, I'll leave you alone and go to the den and pray." He shuts the door. As he walks to the den, he gradually vanishes.

SIXTEEN

Amira dozes off in Q's bed while he's in the shower; she reaches down, grabs her backpack, and notices her phone buzzing. She and Q just finished hooking up. She takes out her phone and sees a text from Detective Porter: "I'm on your block. I'm coming through, to put a little time in."

Still looking at the phone, she thinks, *Bro, you're about thirty minutes late.*

She looks up from her phone and sees Q standing at the end of the bed, dripping wet with a royal blue towel around his waist.

"Who was that?"

She puts her phone on the bed, "Porter, that detective. He wants to come over."

"What did you tell him?" He unwraps the towel and starts drying off his upper body.

"Nothing. What should I tell him?"

"I don't care, do whatever you want." He sits at the end of the bed, still toweling off.

She flips the covers, comes to his side, and begins to gently massage his shoulder, softly saying, "I'm good, you took care of momma. I want to chill with you for the rest of the night."

He shrugs his shoulders to get her off him, then stands up, "Well, you can cancel that. I got other business to tend to. Go ahead and hook up with your boy. Stay in his good graces; we need to keep that connection strong."

Amira sits on the edge of the bed, pissed at how he can discard her so casually after getting together.

He walks into the closet to pick out his fit. He looks over at her, "You thought this meant something? Humph, you or some other trick, it's all the same."

Shaken by his statement, she recovers and tells him, "Aight, I can do that, but I need you to do something for me."

"You know you ain't in no place to be asking any favors." He snarls from the closet. "What is it?"

"A place to stay. My roommate Ciara is moving in with her man, Shady, at the end of the month."

He comes out of the closet, putting on his jeans, "You don't have any homies you can bunk with?"

"Bunk with?"

"Don't play with me, you know what I'm saying."

"All my 'homies' are either at home with family or their man."

He goes to the bathroom to brush his teeth and yells to her, “I ain’t yo man.”

She yells back at him from the bed, saying, "You made sure I understood that I need a few weeks until I get my own place."

He goes to his dresser to get his grill and a blue t-shirt.

“If I do this, I ain’t going to be no step-dad to another nigga’s kid.”

“I’m sure either my mom or Sage’s family will watch him.”

Q, hearing Sage’s name, pauses for a moment. “Have you heard anything?”

She shakes her head no, “The same thing, still in a coma.”

Q shakes his head with fake sympathy. “Damn, this is so fucked up. We were going to blow up together. Kong’s dead, and Big Saint might as well be.” He mumbles, “Casualties of the game.”

Her black bra is hanging from the bedpost. Q tosses it at her, “Get dressed, you've got somewhere you need to be.”

SEVENTEEN

Sage and Sydney, both glowing in their celestial forms, gently float across the hazy, starry night sky. Beneath them, a small, run-down house remains overlooked in the shadows of an unnamed city, with weathered wood siding and rusted bars covering the window, telling stories of neglect.

Sage, still bewildered by what occurred with Jeb Dumas, frantically questions, “Was that real? Did he lose his family? Why did you pull me out?”

“Everything you experienced was genuine; you were placed in this to examine how strong your faith is during times of great tribulation. You accomplished what you needed to do, so there was no reason for you to stay. Do you wish to move forward?”

He asks disbelievingly, “Move forward?” What else do I need to do? I’m not sure I can handle another challenge.” He looks down at the dilapidated neighborhood and questions, “The next test is here, isn’t it?”

“Yes. Once you are in place, you will learn what your test will be. Are you ready?” He smiles at her and nods. Suddenly, a light flashes, and he vanishes.

It's 11:30, and Angel impatiently honks his blue Nissan Sentra while Lil Uzi Vert's "I Wanna Rock" plays. His boys, Loco and Calli, sit in the back smoking a pre-roll. They're at Tony Hassen's house, aka Mite 'T,' a 16-year-old high school dropout and wannabe Ebony Kings recruit, living with his 20-year-old girlfriend, Patience. His brother Shawn and Uncle Gilbert are in prison for distribution.

Patience hears the loud thumping music and the horn. She leans on the couch and peeks out the window. She does not recognize the car and yells to Tony, "There is a white car outside blowing its horn. You know anything bout it?"

He comes out of the bathroom smelling like weed and says, "Yeah, it's Angel. I'm about to go through the process. I'm 'squaring in' with EK."

'Squaring in?' What does that mean?" She yells at him.

He grasped the doorknob, "Jumped in. Bout to make it official. EK all the way."

She seizes his right wrist, pulls him back from the door, and shouts, "Why?"

"They, my niggas, my family, brother, and uncle, are EK; it's in my blood. It's only a minute long. I'll be alright."

"The only blood is yours on the street after they whoop your ass! Don't come back here all beat to hell and think I'm taking care of you!"

He snatches his arm away from her. “That don’t scare me! My brothers got my back!” The car horn blares outside. “I’m out.” He opens the door and shuffles to the car.

Angel leans over and opens the door as he walks to the car. Mite ‘T’ gets in. Angel turns down the music, “What’s up, my boy? You ready?”

Nervously, he answers, “Hell yeah! Ready to get it over and make it real with my bros.”

From the back seat, Loco, giggling, answers, “You don’t sound too sure.” He offers him the pre-roll.

Angel puts the car in drive and takes off. ‘T’ takes a toke.

He passes it back to Loco, who takes a huge hit.

Calli’s sitting in the backseat, quietly listening and absorbing everything in.

“Where’s it going down at?” T asks.

“On the courts at Washington Park, OG Poppy is waiting on us,” Angel answers.

The park is just around the corner, and up the block, they arrive in front of the basketball court. Angel picks up a bottle from the passenger side floor and steps out of the car. He then does a confident, playful stride while holding the bottle overhead, shouting, “Angel Santos EK on deck.”

The court is entirely dark. Loco heads to the power box and switches it on. Only one person is on the court, an older man in his thirties, swinging his arms back and forth, stretching. He has a dark green bandana tied around his neck. After stretching, he raises his right hand in an EK hand stack and says, "Poppy EK on deck." Then, he takes the beer from his hand and takes a large sip.

"Where is the newbie at?" He yells.

T is out of the car and walks cautiously to the court. Calli follows behind. He has pulled up his green bandana covering his mouth and nose.

"Let's go nigga, you wanted this. Now is the time to step up. It's too late to turn back!" Calli shoves him from behind, almost causing him to trip as they walk onto the court.

"You know what I'm sayin?" T goes to the center of the court, and all four surround him. Poppy starts in, "We need to make sure that you EK worthy, that you are going to have that heart to rock out no matter if it's one-on-one or five-on-one. We have no set time limit and rock on until we see what you got. Gun, knife, it don't make no difference, know what I'm sayin. Why you wanna be EK?"

"My uncle and older brother are in the 691 set in N.C. I grew up with EK's they family. It's all I know. I wanna make it legit."

Poppy doesn't respond; he gives a slight head nod to Calli, who's standing behind T. Poppy pulls his cell phone out and starts recording. Calli throws a wild right hook that surprises T in his right jaw. He quickly ducks his head down to protect himself. He falls to the ground. Calli rushes over and smashes him with a solid right cross that lands on his right eye. He is on the ground in the fetal position as Calli and Loco are on top of him, hammering away.

“Fight back nigga! Fight back!” Poppy yells as he continues recording.

Angel repeatedly kicks him in the stomach while T lies on the ground. T yells, “Damn!! Damn!! Hold up!”

Poppy goes over and pulls Calli and Loco off of him and yells, “Chill! Chill! Give him a chance to stand up.” Poppy helps him to his feet. While T is still bent down, feeling his nose because it’s bleeding. Loco runs up to him and knees him in the face with a glancing blow. T tackles Loco to the ground, climbs on top of him starts hammering his face.

“That’s it, my boy! Fight back! Show them niggas what you got!” He yells hysterically, still recording.

Calli runs over and tackles him off of Loco. T lies face down on the court. Loco and Calli get up and viciously kick and stomp on him. He is covered up in the fetal position and again yells, “Aight! Aight! I’m done, dawg!”

Angel watches and takes another swig of the beer. He places the bottle on the ground, runs up, and pushes Calli off first, then Loco. He crouches down over T to shield his body and yells, “Yo, enough! He’s done. You made your point!”

Poppy goes over, picks up the beer bottle, and smashes it on the back of Angel's head. His head is bleeding as he feels the back of it.

"What the hell, Pop? What you do that for?" Angel screams.

Poppy angrily yells, "Don't you ever stop the jump in, know what I'm sayin!? Now get the hell out of the way so they can finish." He pauses, "Better yet, so you can finish."

Angel still crouched over T, "Look at him, man. He ain't nothing but a kid. What does it prove to beat up on a kid?

"He knew what this life is about." He pauses, "Well, if he doesn't get the beatdown, you do."

He motions for Calli and Loco to go over. Both shake their head no. Calli answers, "It's over nigga. Let's go."

Now, furious Poppy pulls out a pistol and puts it directly on the back of Angel's head where the bottle broke, "Since you want to be his guardian angel, you willing to die for him?"

He moves his head from the gun barrel, "My name is Angel."

This pisses him off even more as he screams, "You think this is a joke?? Nigga, EK is my life, my family. I'm willing to die for it! Are you?"

"Not For EK. But I can't let you keep beating on this boy. If it means I have to die tonight to stop it, then I'm ready."

Calli and Loco see the anger building up in Poppy. Loco yells in desperation, "Yo dawg, you ain't got to do this. Let's go home, smoke, and welcome 'T' to the set."

He looks at both of them and points the gun at them, screams, "It's too late for that. I can't have nobody disrespecting me or the set. Know what I'm saying?"

He turns sharply, presses the cold barrel of the gun firmly against the cut in the back of Angel's head, and a spiteful smile forms across his face as he locks eyes with Calli and Loco. Without hesitation, he pulls the trigger.

Everything goes black.

EIGHTEEN

A radiant white door appears in the night sky as Sage's life force drifts toward it. After he passes through, the door gradually disappears. He finds himself in a black void, surrounded by darkness, with no light or sound; it is neither hot nor cold. Sage spins around, observing his surroundings. From afar, he notices a flicker of light, something glowing. It begins to move toward him, and as it nears, he recognizes it as the emissary. Her glow intensifies, illuminating the entire void. Sage asks, "Why are we here?"

Smiling at him, she replies, "You have completed the task. You can now meet the Supremacy."

She softly extends her hand and holds his. Together, they fade from the emptiness and reappear inside a majestic temple. The floors and ceiling are crafted from pristine white marble. On each side, five enormous gold columns stand, with seven-foot-tall candles burning next to each, guiding the eye toward an altar. Behind the altar, three massive bay windows rise ten feet, showcasing a night sky ablaze with countless stars.

The Supremacy sits in the lotus pose and levitates three feet off the floor in front of the throne. His outfit is a long black monk's robe with a hood over his face. He wears a gold cincture around the waist.

The emissary quickly vanishes without a word.

Without opening his eyes, he bellows to Sage in a deep booming voice that echoes through the temple, "Come forward!"

Unexpectedly, Sage senses himself being drawn toward the altar. He is abruptly halted roughly six feet from the Supremacy.

"Why me?"

He opens his pupil less eyes, and they glow brightly. Sage is unable to look at him because of this. In a more subdued tone, "The world today is filled with greed, envy, disease, lust, sloth, hate, and pride, which leads to wars and the threat of war. In your past life, you were very much part of this. Free will has given people a chance to make good and bad decisions. The creator will never take away free will, yet he wants man to honor and worship him. I, as the Supremacy, being delegated as an observer to maintain the balance between good and evil. The current state of the world is rife with corruption, permeating everything from world governments to family life. The creator has decided that the people need a symbol of hope to renew man's faith in the positives of the world today, and Blac Angel is that symbol. Your deeds and words as Blac Angel can bring hope back. Your mother was once a Blac Angel, but she gave it up for love. She is now the earthly mentor. She believed in you even through your deficiencies. During the challenges, you showed fearlessness, devotion, bravery, and fortitude."

Sage has no memory of this. “What challenges?”

“You were placed in two separate and distinctive life-altering circumstances. One tested your devotion and strength under immense pressure. The other tested your willingness for the ultimate sacrifice to give up your life to protect an innocent. Because you passed both circumstances, you now have the chance to receive the gifts given to you and become the Blac Angel. There are a few guidelines you need to follow. You should never use your gifts as Blac Angel for nefarious reasons, personal gain, or profit. If used with ill intent, it can be taken away in an excruciating process.”

“What if I kill someone?”

“If the death is in the protection of innocent life, then you did what had to be done.”

“Let’s start the transformation. You must see things as I do.” The Supremacy seizes his right wrist, letting Sage adopt the lotus pose and levitate above the altar. They face each other, with the Supremacy's eyes closed. Though two feet apart, Sage cannot see the Supremacy's face.

The Supremacy takes hold of both his wrist, and they merge into one. He tells Sage, “Now grab and repeat after me, Dum vivimus vivamus.”

Sage grabs his wrist through the robe. He starts chanting with him. Supremacy begins chanting “Dum vivimus vivamus” over and over.

As they keep chanting, a deep golden aura surrounds them. They raise their voices, making the glow brighter, beaming like a hundred suns. Their bodies shake intensely as they chant, and the Supremacy's eyes are now red. Sage feels an overwhelming heat from his wrist, through his arms and chest, down to his legs. It feels like his whole body is on fire.

<<<<>>>>

In his hospital room, he trembles uncontrollably on the bed, causing his entire body to shudder with intense force. All this trembling sets off the EKG, heart monitors, and ventilator alarms. Two RNs, Jones and Smith, are at the nurse's station drinking coffee and talking. They hear the warnings and rush into Sage's room. Jones is the first one in the room and turns on the light. She rushes over, grabs him by the shoulders, and yells to Smith, "Check the vent and ensure he is getting air."

Smith runs to the other side of the bed, "On it." She pushes some buttons on the ventilator and yells, "It's good."

He is still shaking ferociously. In a panic, Jones struggles to hold him down and yells, "What's causing this?"

While messing with the EKG, RN Smith yells frantically, "I don't know. Everything is reading normal on the EKG!"

The trembling slowly begins to subside. As his body calms down, Jones stands back up. "What the hell was that?"

Smith is now resetting the heart monitor and shrugs. "I don't know. It would have registered if it were a seizure or a heart attack. I've been a nurse for over ten years and have never seen anything like that."

Jones is adjusting the blankets as Sage, drenched in sweat, lies peacefully in bed. She then moves to the ventilator and says, "We need to review the readings from all the monitors for the last thirty minutes to identify any discrepancies."

Smith nods her head in agreement.

At the temple, the altar is bathed in a dark evergreen light. The aura surrounds Sage and the Supremacy as they sit in the lotus pose. They are no longer chanting. The Supremacy's eyes now share the same evergreen glow as the aura.

The aura around them gradually fades, and the green glow vanishes. The Supremacy's eyes return to their light white brightness.

He releases Sage's wrist, causing his eye to glow more intensely. He says, "It's your time." The Supremacy lifts out of the lotus pose and ascends vertically. It enlarges to twenty feet and hovers above the altar. Instantly, two coal-black wings, each eight feet long, emerge from his back. He then flies through the open ring at the temple's center into the dark sky. Sage extends his right hand, revealing a six-inch Crusader's cross decorated with small, clear crystals all over it. As he departs, his spirit begins to fade from the temple.

At the hospital, Sage remains still in bed, surrounded by the steady beeping of monitors and equipment. Suddenly, a sharp female voice rings loudly in his mind, shouting, “It’s Time!” His eyes fly open, filled with shock and anticipation.

THE AWAKENING

Awake, O sleeper and arise from the dead, and Christ will shine on you

Isaiah 60:1

NINETEEN

Sage wakes up as the nurse checks his EKG readings.

Groggily, he turns to the right to look at her. From the corner of her eye, she sees he's awake. "Okay! Wow! You awake! This is incredible."

He tries to speak, but his voice is barely audible. He whispers, "How long have I been here?" Then he tries to sit up in bed. She stops adjusting the machine and holds him down, "Slow down, you've been out for six months. You need to take your time. There is no rush."

He doesn't fight it and lies back down, and underneath the covers, he feels something. It's the crusaders' cross. He slowly pushes to the edge of the bed, and it falls to the floor.

Stunned, she picks it up, looks at it, and places it on top of the EKG. "How did this get here? Is this yours?" She inquires.

Sage stares at it on top of the machine. He nods his head. He still doesn't know what the cross means. Everything that happened in the coma was real.

"You must've been having a crazy dream. The night shift crew said you were trembling like you were in an earthquake."

"What are you talking about? What happened last night?" He whispers

"In the morning, past down, they reported you were shaking intensely last night, causing the machines to go off. After about ten minutes, it suddenly stopped. They checked you, and everything appeared normal. You were sweating as if you'd run a marathon. There must be some link between what happened last night and you waking up this morning. She then looks at the cross and suggests, "Maybe your family brought it with them when they came and prayed over you."

He knows that's not true. In a strained voice, he screeches, "My family! Where is my phone? I want to call them."

"Stop talking, you haven't spoken in six months, give yourself time." The nurse walks down to the end of the bed, and a sealed plastic bag is on a desk. Inside the bag are his wallet, belt, and phone. I will give it to you but you are only allowed to text. He grabs the phone, turns it on, and texts his mother.

The nurse leaves, "I will give you some privacy." She walks out of the room.

Sydney's home at the kitchen table, drinking a homemade energy drink. Her phone rings on the table. She looks at it and smiles.

With an excited yet calm tone, she texts, "*Welcome back, son. You got my message.*"

They quickly began texting back and forth,

"Everything that I experienced was real?"

"Yes. Now we need to tell your father."

"How come you never talked about it before?"

"*If I told you, would you believe me? I know you got a million questions. We can talk about it when you get home. I need to call your father to tell him the good news. How do you feel?"*

"*To be honest, confused, weak, lost.*"

"Has a doctor seen you yet?" She asks as she walks to her room.

"No, I just woke up a few minutes ago. I was talking to the nurse, and she mentioned my family."

"Stephon and I will be up there in a few hours. Love you, see you later."

<<<<>>>>

Stephon and Sydney arrive at his room. Sage is sitting in bed, eating a bowl of tomato soup and a cheese sandwich. Stephon is surprised to see him so fully alert and active.

With a big smile, he rushes up and hugs him. 'The Lord truly works in mysterious ways.' "It is so good to have you back."

Sage puts the cheese sandwich down and answers quietly. They did an MRI a few minutes ago, and if everything checks out fine. I can come home today."

Sydney sees the crusaders cross on the EKG machine. She discreetly approaches it and slips it into her purse.

Still stunned by Sage's rapid recovery, Stephon remarks, "This is a miracle. I can't believe you are coming home."

Sydney walks back to Stephon and says, "We got a lot to talk about when we get home."

TWENTY

They're all sitting at the dining room table. Stephon is at the head, with Sydney to his right and Sage to his left. Sage looks at Sydney and asks, "You told us to wait until we get home. What's the big secret?"

She reaches out and holds his hand. "Before we get into that, I need to tell you Cameron was killed during the accident, shot in the head just like you were."

A lump forms in Sage's throat. Deep down, he already knew, but hearing it makes it real. His eyes water as he asks, "Do the police know who did it?"

Stephon answers, "They questioned us about it, but they say they don't have any suspects. They want to question you."

With tears in his eyes, he looks at his mom, and he reminisces about Kong and everything they've been through growing up. "I need to do this for Kong. What do you need to tell us?"

Her purse is on the table. She reaches into it, pulls out the cross medallion, and places it in front of them.

Stephon picks it up and examines it with a quizzical look. He notices the jewels embedded in it. "Where did you get it? Why are you showing it to us?"

He tosses it back onto the table. She looks at him and replies, "It's not mine, it's Sage's."

Sage reaches over, picks it up, startled replies, "What am I supposed to do with this?"

She looks at him and says, "This is the key to you becoming the Blac Angel."

"Blac Angel? Who is Blac Angel?" Stephon asked, confused.

She responds, "Blac Angel represents hope and love. Our son experienced a spiritual awakening during his coma. With that cross, he can become a warrior, or some call a superhero," she explains.

Stephon, with an incredulous look, "What are you talking about? How do you know this?"

She stands up, steps back from the table, and gradually levitates about five feet off the ground. Both of them gaze upward at her, hovering above the table. Stephon's eyes and mouth are wide with shock at the sight, while Sage wears a broad smile, delighted that everything during the coma was real.

She looks down at them, "I was once a Blac Angel." She then gracefully floats back down and sits at the table.

"Once? Why did you give it up?" Sage asks.

Smiling, she looks at Stephon and answers, "Love. I fell in love with your father. He was the man I wanted to spend the rest of my life with, and I didn't want anything to get in the way. I knew he could be great through his ministry and wanted to be with him."

Stephon is still astonished by what he has just been told, "Why didn't you say anything?"

"Why would I need to? That part of my life I thought was over forever. The Supremacy messaged me. He believed now is a good time for a Blac Angel to appear."

Stephon asks, "Why Sage?"

She looks at Sage, "The life he led before the accident was not typical for a spiritual warrior. He was part of a world caught up in materialism and selfishness, yet he also displayed fearlessness and bravery. Those characteristics are qualities of a Blac Angel, and I saw this as a chance for redemption. The Supremacy challenged him to see if he is worthy of being the Blac Angel."

Sage grabs the cross off the table and holds it before his face, staring at the jewels, "How is this the key?"

"When you hold it and say the chant, you will transform into the Blac Angel."

He twirls it in his hand, "Chant?"

She answers, "Yes, to activate the cross, you must say the right words."

Stephon, "What kinds of powers does he have?"

"He will possess super strength, the ability to fly, slow down time, heal himself when injured, and perform astral projection. As he gains experience, his powers will become even more powerful."

Sage hears this and is excited about the chance.

Stephon's mind is spinning from everything he hears. He looks at Sage and asks, "Are you done with that gang?"

Sage turns and looks at Stephon in the eyes. "I'm done, I swear. Before the accident, I was caught up in the world, confused, and lost. I had my priorities focused on the wrong things. While in the hospital, I had a life-altering experience; I wasn't sure if it was real. Now, I know it was. I have a second chance at life and have been given a gift to make a difference."

He looks at his mother, "What's next?"

"Well, you need to train. In about a week or two, we will start. I want to make sure you are physically able to handle the transformation."

Sage is anxious but understands. He grabs his phone and starts texting. He asks, "Have y'all seen Aiden lately?"

Stephon quickly answers, "No. Amira doesn't didn't bring him around much while you were in the hospital. The last time was about two months ago. She was with that thug Q coming to see you in the hospital."

"I'm texting her. I want to see my son."

Sydney picks up the cross medallion and puts it into her purse. She then stands and says, "I'm about to start dinner." She looks at Sage and adds, "To celebrate your first day back, you can have anything you want. Do you have any requests?"

"Yep, spaghetti, and meatballs with garlic bread."

"You got it, I need to go to the store to pick up a few things."

Stephon stands up and tells her, "I will ride with you."

<<<<>>>>

Sage is lying on the couch playing a game while they are at the store. There is a knock on the door. He opens it, and a man he does not know is standing there. He is wearing khakis and a white golf shirt.

"What's up?" Sage asks.

"I'm Detective Porter with the Elk City PD Gang Unit." He flashes the badge attached to the left side of his belt.

"You, Sage Reed?"

"Yeah, What's up?"

"Is it okay if I come in? I got a few questions I would like to ask you."

Sage isn't very friendly with cops because of his 187 days. He stays silent as he opens the door and nods for Porter to come in.

He walks in, "Is it okay if I sit down?" Once again, Sage motions with his head. Sage remains standing and leans against the wall bookcase.

“I need to ask you about the morning Cameron ‘Kong’ King was killed. Do you remember anything about it?”

“Cuz I was in a coma for six months. What do you think I remember?” he replies snarkily.

“Do you got a problem with me?”

Sage snaps back, “I got a problem with all po-po.”

Sarcastically, Porter responds, “Look, cuz whatever problem you got with the police, it don’t have anything to do with me.”

Sage thinks about his comment and his new outlook about life calms down, and in a relaxed tone, answers, “You're right, my bad, I don’t remember a thing. I was asleep in the car when he was killed.”

“Are you with the 187s?”

“Why?”

Frustrated with his attitude, Detective Porter yells at him, “Look, cuz I have to ask! This could be some kind of gang hit or something.”

“Cuz this ain’t got nothing to do with no gang thing.” Sage replies back sarcastically.

“How would you know if you don’t remember anything?”

Stumped by the question, Sage gets off the bookcase, walks to the door, and tells him, “I told you everything, I know. It’s time for you to go playa.”

Detective Porter stands up, “If I find out you're lying to me, I’ll be back, and next time I won’t be as polite.”

Sage smirks at him as he leaves.

Detective Porter pulls out his phone in the car and texts Q, *He doesn’t know a thing.*

TWENTYONE

DAMN, you home? *Me and Aiden are on the way* Amira texted to Sage.

After the meal, Stephon leans back in his chair and tells Sage, "Normally, there are no phones at the table, but since this is your first night home from the hospital, we can make an exception."

Sage is pleased to see his father relaxed and calm. He smiles and shakes his head to acknowledge his comment.

He looks at his mother and jokes, "That was the best spaghetti I've had all year."

Smiling, she replies, "This is the only spaghetti you have had all year. Is Amira coming by?"

"Yeah, that's who I was texting."

Sydney goes around him and picks up his plate. "You going to be alright?" She is concerned about how he might be with Amira.

"Why wouldn't I be?" The doorbell rings.

"I got it." She quickly drops the plates in the sink.

Sage and Stephon get up from the table, walk to the living room, and sit on the gold couch.

Sydney opens the door. When Aiden sees his dad, he runs into the house and hugs him.

Sydney smiles as she watches him run into the house. She opens the door wider so Amira can come in, “Hello, Amira. Come in.”

Amira walks in, goes over to Sage, and hugs him. In an ecstatic tone, “It is so good to see you again! I didn’t know if you were ever going to wake up.”

Aiden sits down, glances at Sage’s messy face and hair, and says, "You need a haircut. Were you dead?”

Sage chuckles, “You do too. We can get one this weekend. No. I wasn’t dead; I was in a deep sleep, but I'm back now. I missed you, boy.” He hugs him again.

“I missed you, too, Dad.”

Stephon rises from the couch and says, "It was nice seeing everyone, but I need to begin preparing my sermon for the Sunday service.” He hugs Aiden and adds, "See you later, young man.”

“Okay, Papa.” Stephon goes upstairs.

Sage looks at Amira, “How are you doing?”

Sydney, sensing that they need to talk alone, walks over to Aiden, “You hungry, sweetie? Granny got some leftover spaghetti.” He shakes his head yes, and she grabs his hand, and they go to the kitchen.

Amira looks back at him, takes a deep breath, and in a low tone, answers, “Things have been better. Aiden is having some problems at school.” Amira and Sage watch as they walk away.

“What kind of problems?” Sage inquires

“Not listening to the teacher, not doing school work, you know, normal boy stuff. I’m hoping it's just a phase.”

“I’m back, and I will set him straight.”

Amira gives him a peculiar look, “I don’t know what it is...but something’s different about you.”

Ignoring her comment, answers, “He’s my son, and I need to be there for him.”

She pauses and looks away from him, “I moved in with Q about two months ago till I can get back on my feet.”

“Aiden is not staying with Q,” he declares defiantly. “I can’t tell you what to do, but my son is not staying there. He can stay with me here.”

“Q didn’t want to keep Aiden. Everything works out with you being home now. I know you and Q are boys from the 187s. What’s with the hate?”

“I'm not the same man you knew before. You know what the 187s are about. That ain’t no place for a kid to be around. He can spend the night here, and we’ll hang out and get to know each other again. Get our haircuts tomorrow morning.”

Sydney's busy loading up the dishwasher. Amira stands up, "Let me go home and pack his bag." She walks over to the kitchen, where Aiden is playing with his spaghetti.

She walks over to the table, bends down, and tilts his head to make sure he looks at her. "You will stay with your dad tonight. Is that okay?"

He excitedly shakes his head up and down in agreement. Sage is happy that his son is cool with staying with him. Sydney, hearing the conversation, stops wiping down the counter and looks over at Sage, "Aiden is staying with us?"

He answers her back, "I knew you would be happy to have your only grandson stay."

She smiles, "Of course, my grandson is always welcome."

Amira stands up and looks at Sage, "I need to go home and pack. I'll be back later."

She walks to the front door as Sage follows behind. Before she opens the door, she turns to him. "You are not the same man as before. I don't know how you change, but I can tell you're different."

"I almost died. That would change anybody, even you."

She opens the door, shakes her head, agreeing with him, "That's probably it."

In the car, driving home, Amira gets on the phone.

She calls Q, "I'm busy. What's up?" Q yells.

He, Shady, and another banger, Blade, are packaging some trees.

“Sage is back home. I just left his house.”

Excited, Q yells, “Big Saint, my dawg is back!! I need to holla at my boy to get this rolling even bigger. You coming through later?”

“I didn’t plan to.” She answers.

“Change your plans.” He hangs up.

“This fool doesn’t give a shit about me.” She mumbles to herself

Q quickly starts texting.

<<<<>>>>

Sage is lying on the couch while Aiden is watching a music video on TV.

His phone pings in the kitchen. Sage grabs the remote and pauses it, “Go get my phone.”

Aiden quickly gets up, runs to the kitchen, gets the phone, and drops it on his dad's chest.

He hits the remote to play the video and looks at his phone. It’s a text from Q, *Big Saint! I heard you back home. When you coming through?*

He drops the phone back on his chest and thinks, *Amira, she never could keep her mouth shut. I ain’t ready to see this fool yet.*

TWENTYTWO

Sage's phone alarm *buzzes*. He rolls over and picks it up to turn it off. It's 7 a.m., and he and Aiden plan to go to the barbershop. He wants to arrive early to dodge the Saturday morning crowd.

"Aiden, get up!" He shakes his shoulders to wake him. Aiden shrugs him off. "Come on, boy, let's go." He pulls him up by his arms from the bed. Aiden whines. He realizes keeping Aiden with him will be more challenging than expected. Frustrated by his son's crankiness, he gets up and heads downstairs. Stephon and Sydney are already in the kitchen, eating breakfast.

"Good morning, son. Where's Aiden?" Sydney asks.

"Still asleep," he says, rubbing his nappy afro with his right hand. "I'm trying to get us a cut this morning before the Saturday rush."

Sydney gets up from the table, "Let me go ahead and get that baby up."

"You've been home for a few days now, son, and I noticed you haven't been out. Everything okay?" Stephon asks.

He nods his head, "Yes, "I'm getting there, feeling better each day. Whatever energy or power I got while in that coma, I can feel in me. I need to lay low until the time is right."

"I can drop you and Aiden at the barber. If you don't feel comfortable about driving yet."

Sydney and Aiden are coming down the stairs. Aiden drowsily walks over to the table and drops down in the chair. She goes over to the cabinet and grabs a blue cereal bowl.

"Go ahead and get dressed. I will get Aiden ready."

"Thanks, mom." He looks over at his dad, "I feel good enough to drive."

Sage has been getting his haircut at Monte's since he was Aiden's age. He drives around the back of the small white wooden building and parks. Monte's Barbershop is a neighborhood institution. The building is as old as Stephon. Monte Sr started the shop and passed it on to his son, Monte Jr.

Monte's Barbershop is painted on the glass door. Sage and Aiden get out, walk around to the front, and see the broken old-school red-and-blue barber pole on the porch. Sage opens the door, and the antique bell at the top rings as he enters.

Monte Jr sits in the barber's chair, farther from the door, texting on his phone. When Sage walks in, he happily jumps out of the chair and yells, "Look who is back from the dead. My homie Big Saint!" He gives him a big brotherly hug.

"It's good seeing you, Big Saint!"

"It's good being seen, J Dawg." He looks around the shop, "I see you and your old man still doing your thing."

"He'll be here in a few hours; he can't put in the hours like he used to. He looks at Sage's nappy afro and beard, "Damn Saint, how long it's been?"

"Six months." He pauses and continues, "I was down for six months." He motions for Aiden to come over and sit in the chair.

"Hook my boy and me up."

"What kinda cut you want for him?" Aiden jumps into the barber chair. Sage goes over to the row of black vinyl chairs on the other wall and sits.

"Fade the sides and sponge twist the top."

He puts the black barber apron around Aiden's neck and turns on the clippers.

"Six months! Damn, that's a long time! You were in a coma? What was that like?"

He chuckles softly, a gentle, bittersweet sound, and slowly shakes his head, as if trying to clear the confusion in his eyes. He looks into the distance, searching for the right words, a slight furrow in his brow. "I don't know where to start; it feels like a never-ending dream."

The bell on top of the door rings, and in walks Kong's old girlfriend, Brigette, who holds her son Luke's hand.

Astonished, she releases Luke's hand and screams, "Oh my God!"

She rushes over to him, and he quickly stands up. They embrace, and she holds him tightly, as if she never wants to let go.

Crying on his right shoulder, she whispers in his right ear, "I can't believe you're here. It is so good to see you."

They both sit down. Luke sits on the other side of his mom. She reaches into her clutch and gives him her phone to keep him busy. Sage, now caught up in her emotional state, begins to tear up.

Seeing him for the first time reminds her of Kong; she's whispering, "I miss him so much."

Sage slowly shakes his head, "I miss him too. He was my brother."

"You were the last one to see him alive. What happened?"

The phone rings, and J Dawg begins to talk while cutting Aiden's hair.

"I would never lie to you. I don't know. I don't remember anything about that night. I was pretty much asleep the whole time we did the pickup. What did the cops tell you?"

She looks up at J Dawg, who is arguing with whomever he is talking to.

"They ain't doing shit. They say the same thing every time I call. It's an open investigation; they will contact me if something changes."

She again looks up at J. Dawg, who is still on the phone talking. He has stopped cutting, turned his back on them, and is almost whispering now.

Leaning toward Sage, she whispers, "Word is Q put the hit out."

Sage's head snaps back with shock, "WHY?"

"You didn't know this, but Kong was an informant for the cops. That run y'all were doing was gonna be his last. Q somehow found out he was a snitch, and I guess he wanted to do you, too. She whispers even lower, scared, "You did not hear this from me."

He looks at her and holds her right hand for comfort, "Say no, mo. Who was Kong's contact with the police?"

"I think his name was Detective Porter? Why?"

"That's the same cop who came by my house questioning me. That is too big a coincidence. I need to talk with him again."

She looks at him worried, "Please don't do anything crazy. If he did the hit, he might try it again."

J Dawg hangs up the phone. He looks over at Big Saint, "That was my girl, she was trippin about some child support. He turns the clippers back on, "Don't worry, I'm hooking your boy up."

Big Saint acknowledges him with a head nod. He thinks *Q and Porter are working together?*

TWENTYTHREE

Stephon pulls into his driveway after another long day of landscaping. He is tired and looking forward to a hot dinner and a shower. Sage and Sydney sit in the candle-lit living room in the yoga lotus pose.

They are facing each other, eyes shut. She tells him calmly, "I need you to find your center, control your breathing, and relax. If your mind and spirit are strong, your body will follow."

Stephon, annoyed for some unknown reason, notices this and intentionally slams the door. Sage and Sydney are startled and brought back to the present.

Stephon walks in and takes a seat on the couch, remarking, "We've been married for over twenty years, and I never knew you did yoga."

"Haven't you learned anything in the last few days? There was a lot you didn't know about me?" Maintaining the position, she continues, "It's not just yoga, it's a relaxation technique to help your son prepare for the transition to the Blac Angel."

He asks in an exasperated tone. "I keep hearing about this Blac Angel. What exactly is the Blac Angel?"

She gets up and shuffles past him, "I can show you better than I can tell you."

Both Stephon and Sage look at each other, puzzled.

She has the crusader cross in her hand.

"Let's go to the backyard."

Sage and Stephon get up and follow her into the kitchen through the sliding door to the back porch.

She turns to Sage and says, "Here, put this on." She places the cross around his neck.

He looks her in the eyes. He is filled with mixed emotions, excitement, fear, and anxiety all rolled into one.

She looks at his outfit: a plain white t-shirt, gray baller shorts, and gray sliders. "Maybe you should take off your shirt."

"Is that really necessary?" Stephon asks in a sarcastic tone.

Sage takes off the shirt and takes two deep breaths.

Repeat after me, "Dum vivimus vivamus, and keep repeating it."

He gradually starts growing taller and stronger. His arms, legs, chest, and abdominals begin gaining muscle mass. As he grows, the cross glows so brightly that it is almost blinding. The crystal jewels in the cross start burning. The cross slowly stops glowing, and he stops growing. The whole process takes thirty seconds. He is now about 6'2 "and has gained 60 pounds of muscle.

Stephon looks at him, stupefied, with his mouth wide open, "What the hell? I'd never would have believed it if I didn't see it with my own eyes."

"How do you feel?" She asks, smiling.

"Strong...Powerful." He flexes his arms and hands over his chest and legs.

"I didn't know what would happen, but I didn't expect this. I'm ready to do this!" He yells out.

"Yeah! It looks like it! Boy, you the real deal." Stephon comments back, almost as excited.

"Slow down, you two. He isn't there yet. He's still got some work to put in. We must ensure he is physically fit and mentally strong. He needs to be strong in mind and body. The stronger he is, the stronger Blac Angel will be."

Sage flexes his arms in the classic muscleman pose. "I guess it was good I took off the shirt."

Sydney stands there with her eyes closed while Stephon still gawks over Sage's new and improved physique.

"Can you hear me?" The female voice asks in Sage's head.

"Mom? Yes, I hear you," Sage answers back. She's astral projected into his head.

I'm testing to make sure our bond remains intact now that you're back in the physical world. I can access your subconscious whenever you need me to. You can think of me as your co-pilot.

Her eyes open back up, and she is back in her body. They smile at each other over the inside info about the astral projection.

Sydney looks at Sage with a solemn expression. "You know, once you put yourself out, there is no turning back; you will make enemies who are going to come after you."

"With prayer and your guidance and training, the Lord will take care of him," Stephon says.

Sage, confident with his new and improved physique, cockily replies, "I'm ready."

<<<<>>>>

Reverend Reed stands confidently at the pulpit, gazing over the overflowing congregation. In the front row, right in the middle, Sydney and Aiden sit attentively, their eyes fixed on the reverend. The church is bustling with life, filled to capacity with eager listeners. "I want to thank everyone for joining us this morning. Normally, at this time, we get a selection from the choir; however, today, I would like to welcome back a church member who has been gone, but not forgotten. Through your prayers and the grace of God, he is now back with us. It's my distinct privilege to welcome back my pride and joy, my son Sage." He extends his right arm toward the back of the church. The congregation turns around and looks at Sage sitting in the back pew.

"Come on up here, son." He gestures with his right hand for him to come forward.

He waves Stephon off, and the congregation starts to clap, encouraging him to go to the pulpit. Sage meekly smiles, gets up, and begins walking to the front. As he slowly strolls towards the pulpit, more people stand up to give him an ovation. He puts his head down in embarrassment. At the pulpit, his father has stepped aside from the podium to allow him to say a few words.

Sage steps up and looks out at the congregation, and much to his surprise, he sees Candace. Tears are forming in her eyes as she happily applauds his appearance. She pulls out her phone and starts to video him. He looks directly at her and smiles. Speaking into the microphone, he is joyful and grateful. "Thank you, thank you, I don't have much to say. I am overcome with emotion from my father's glorious introduction. I want to thank everybody for your prayers while I was away. Being in that coma was a blessing in disguise. It showed me how important life is and how it can be taken away in a moment. I know a lot of you know I was living a lie, a phony façade, before the accident, a hypocrite. Singing and praising God on Sundays, and that same night doing the devil's work in the streets. I stand before you as a new person, a changed man. God has blessed me with a new start, and I will do everything I can to be the man God, my family, and this church will be proud of. I want to end with this: nothing is promised to anybody. Give your family and friends their flowers while everybody is still around to enjoy them. May God continue to bless you all."

The congregation gives him a standing ovation. A female voice yells loudly, "Sing something."

He recognizes the voice and looks at Candace, she laughs because she put him on the spot. He leans down into the microphone and answers, "I haven't sung since the accident. Maybe next time." He steps down from the pulpit and sits with his mom and son.

"Thank you, son, for those inspirational words. Smiling, he continues, 'Next time, we're going to hold you to that. Now, a selection from our choir."

<<<<>>>>

The service is over. A circle of church members surrounds Sage and Aiden; they are making small talk and welcoming him back. Candace spots Sage and is making her way to him. He excuses himself from the group, grabs Aiden's hand, and walks over to her.

"Aiden, I want you to meet a good friend. This is Candace."

"Good friend?' Okay. I like that." They shake hands. She looks at him with tears forming in her eyes. Still shaking hands, she pulls him in. "Give me a hug." They have a close embrace. She takes her phone out, “Turn around,” she whispers to him. Just as he does, she takes a selfie.

Sage, irritated by all the pictures, “Do you really need to do this now?”

“I have always got to be promoting. If you are going to sing, get used to it.”

Switching up on him, she excitedly asks, “Why didn’t you tell me you were home from the hospital?”

He looks down at Aiden, “Can you go find your Nana? I want to talk to Candace.”

“Okay.” He quickly takes off.

He looks back at her, “I didn’t know I needed to. I was under the impression this is a business deal only.”

“We went out once, and I got a lot going on, but I did miss you and want to see where this can go.”

He looks around and notices the church is almost empty. “Can you give me a ride home?”

Surprised by the question, “Um, yeah, sure.”

“Let me tell my people.” He walks to the Reverend’s car. Aiden is already in the back seat, and Stephon and Sydney are in the driver's and passenger seats. He bends down at the driver's door, “Candace is giving me a ride home. I will see you later.”

“Alright, son, have a good time,” Stephon replies as he closes the window and backs the car out.

Candace is in her car, and he jumps in. As she drives away, his phone dings from a text.

It's from Q. *Yo, bro, why you not answering my texts? If there is a prob, we can work it out man-to-man. Come through.*

He stares at the text deep in thought. *I can't keep avoiding him, it.*

On my way, he texts back.

"I need to make a stop before we go home." He tells Candace.

"Where?"

"A former partner of mine. I need to talk with him about something important." He states in a quiet determination.

TWENTYFOUR

***"Candace,* there's something** you should know," Sage says quietly. She keeps her eyes on the road and asks without looking at him, "What is it?"

"I'm in the 187s."

She jams on the brakes in the middle of driving. Yells as she looks at him, "You a gangbanger!"

"I'm quitting, that's why we're going. I'm letting my boy know I'm out." He was not expecting such a striking reaction.

A little shaken by the news, she asks, "Which way?"

"Go straight, then make a right at the light." She takes off.

"Why are you quitting?"

The question causes him to pause. He can't tell her about Blac Angel and everything he went through while in the coma. She would never believe him.

She stops at the traffic light and looks at him, who then meets her gaze with steady eyes. He responds softly, saying, "When I was in the hospital, I experienced something I can't quite explain. I know GOD is real, and he's the only reason I am still here today."

She makes the right turn and drives down the street. "It is the gray house on the right at the end of the cul-de-sac."

He continues, "To show my gratitude. I can't go back to the life I was living. He didn't bring me back so I could return to being a thug. Dropping out of the 187s is a big move for me to become a better man. I will start spending time with the people who really matter, family and real friends." He points to the gray house on the street, "It's right here."

She parks in front of the house. He turns and looks over at it. A few new cameras have been added. He takes out his phone and texts, '*I'm outside.* His nerves kick in as he sits there, staring at the trap.

She looks over at him, hearing the sincerity in his voice, "I believe you. You're not the same when we went on our date." She pauses, "You ever kill anyone?"

The question brings him back. He snaps at her, "Don't ever ask nobody that, especially around here!" He then laughs, "I'm messing with you." He switches back to serious, "That was my initiation to the set." He opens the door, "Let me take care of this. Don't go anywhere."

<<<<>>>>

Sage walks up to the house, and the front door quickly opens. Q stands there with his pet snake, Casper, draped over his shoulder.

Sage is surprised by the sight; he had forgotten all about the snake.

Q pushes open the front gate and yells, "Big Saint! Come in, homey!"

He walks in, Q turns around, and goes to the kitchen, "I was feeding Casper. Let me put him away." He pulls the deep black snake from around his neck and places it in the cage by the back door.

"Sit down, Big Saint!" he yells from the kitchen. Sage sits down on a dark green leather couch. He looks around the room and notices Q's gotten some new furniture. The whole house is a lot cleaner.

"I see you upgrading."

"Yeah, your baby's momma was about to move in." Q stands at the edge of the kitchen, leaning on the doorframe. "With you back home, ya'all can do your thing now."

Sage chuckles and shakes his head, "Naw dawg, you got her. My family ain't having any part of that. I got my boy, though."

"Whatever. Big Saint! Welcome back! Bro!" He walks up to him and gives him a brotherly hug. Q offers his hand to do the 187 handshake. Sage responds by putting his in his pockets.

"I'm not Big Saint, no mo. Don't call me that."

Q offended drops his hand, “Yo, what you ain’t down with the 187s?”

“No, I came by to let you know, man to man. I’m done.”

Q sits down at the weed table, picks up his Glock pistol, and starts fiddling with it. He leans towards Sage. “I figured something was up when you ghosted my texts. Is this about what happened to Kong?”

He turns toward Q from the couch, “I’d be capping if I didn’t say it hasn’t messed with me. I was in the hospital for six months fighting for my life.” He pauses briefly, “While in that coma, I experienced something you will never understand. This money and power you crave doesn’t mean nothing in God’s eye.”

Q responds, “You come out of the coma all holy and sanctified? You're going to yell Bible verses to me like your pops?”

Angered by his attitude, Sage stands up and yells, “This ain’t got nothing to do with my father! I almost got killed doing that pickup for you!”

Q steps to him angrily and towers over him, and grumbles, “Big Saint, check your tone.”

“I told you that’s not my name!” Sage angrily yells back.

“What!! What!! You got a problem?!” Q yells at Sage, challenging him. He snatches Sage by his shirt off the couch. “Do something about it, punk!” He throws Sage toward the weed table, knocking it over. Sage quickly springs to his feet, charging at Q with raging fury, fists clenched and eyes burning with rage. But Q remains unshaken, calmly raising his Glock, a cold smile on his lips as he aims it directly at Sage's forehead. Q shakes his head and replies arrogantly, "Yeah, that's what I thought. You ain't got no heart. Without your boy Kong having your back, you soft as Charmin. Nigga, what happened to you? Kong was the cost of being in the game. I knew that joining the Marines, there was a chance I could be taken out while over in the sandbox. I did two tours in Iraq during the war. I was the lead vehicle in a security convoy. My Hummer ran over an IED, and two of my partners were blown up. I didn't get scared and quit; that's not what a real man does. I can't even count how many firefights I was in. I'm lucky to be alive. I'm in these streets just like you. Nobody will ever punk me. I'll be laid up beside Kong before that happens!"

Sage straightens himself up and shakes his head, seeing that Q ain't getting it. "Aight, bro, whatever you say, I got somebody waiting. I'm out." He gets up, straightens his shirt, and goes to the door.

Q slyly replies, 'You know if you aren't with the 187s, you need to disappear?'

"What?" Sage questions with a twisted look on his face.

"You know too much, and if you ain't with us, you against us."

“What are you trying to say?” Sage asks in an agitated tone.

“It would be a bad deal if you ended up like Kong.” He tells him in a calm but sinister tone.

In a similar tone, Sage answers, “I hear you.” Walking out the door to the car, he thinks *This ain’t over.*

TWENTYFIVE

Candace is in her car, talking on the phone, "I will be on the nine o'clock flight tonight." Sage approaches the car, reaches down, and pops the lock. She then says, "I'll call you back later," and quickly ends the call.

"What took you so long?" She questions as she starts up the car.

He gets in, "I'm sorry. It was tense. He's going to be a problem." She takes off and drives around the cul-de-sac to turn around.

"Tense? That doesn't sound good."

"It went about how I expected."

"What's next?" She asks.

"Not sure. I've got some things I'm working on."

They come to the stoplight, "Make the right here."

She looks at him, "You scared?"

"I can't be scared of no man. If he comes at me, he will be dealt with." He answers arrogantly. She feels a mix of surprise and excitement from his assertive tone.

Wanting to lighten the mood, she changes the topic: "When are you going to start singing again?"

He hadn't considered it since arriving home. After a moment, he replies, "I don't know, I haven't thought about it. Maybe sing with the choir and see what happens."

He pauses, unsure if he should ask, "What's up with you and me?"

They pull up to his house. She looks at him, smiles slyly, "Let's just see what happens. I have been talking to someone."

Without hesitation, he asks, "Was that who you were talking to on the phone?"

Slyly, she answers, "Maybe."

"Have you hooked up with him yet?"

Shocked that he would be so bold, "Slow your roll, we ain't there with each other, the nerve." She chuckles to herself.

"I'm just tryin to see where I fit in."

"Look, I'm going down to Dallas. I don't know when I'm coming back. I'll hit you up when I'm back in town."

Q and how to deal with his has him distracted, he answers, "Cool."

She leans and hugs him, "I will text you when I return to town. Goodnight."

Sage enters his house, finding it empty. The furniture remains pushed against the wall. He sits on the couch, contemplating Q's suppressed threat. The silent room motivates him to meditate. He moves to the floor, assuming the lotus pose, closing his eyes. He takes ten deep breaths, inhaling through his nose and exhaling through his mouth. This practice has uncovered a calmness and peacefulness within him that he had never known.

The door swings open unexpectedly, and Sydney enters, sweating from her five-mile run in the afternoon. She is happily surprised to see him practicing the lotus pose. Without hesitation, she heads to the kitchen to grab a premade energy drink from the fridge and sits down at the table.

She quietly sits there at the table, not wanting to interrupt him.

After about fifteen minutes of silence, he returns. Sydney inquires, "What inspired this?"

He gets up, walks to the kitchen, and sits across from her, "I went to see Q after service today, and he told me. It would be bad if I ended up like Kong."

"Is he threatening you?" She asks, sipping on her drink.

Slowly nodding his head, "He told me to watch my back. I told him I was done with the 187s."

"You think he was serious?"

"Hell yeah! The 187s and the Marines were the only things he cared about, and the Marines kicked him out. I'm ready to be the Blac Angel. I need to be prepared when he comes after me."

She takes a big drink from the bottle and looks him in the eyes.

"I'm your mother, and I do love you, but our relationship will change once we start. You need to be ready for the biggest physical and mental challenge you've ever faced. This isn't about being your mother; I will be your Master trainer, whose only job is to prepare you to become the Blac Angel, she emphasizes, *By whatever means necessary."*

Without missing a beat, he answers, "Let's do whatever it takes. I'm ready."

She gets up from the table and walks to the stairs. "Tomorrow morning at five, we start."

TWENTYSIX

The Clouds are moving in, Sage and Sydney jog on the sidewalk side by side as traffic whizzes by. Sage is huffing and puffing as he trots along, trying to keep pace with his mom. They run four miles to Bearclaw Park, once around it, and back home. They have circled the park and are now headed back.

Thunder echoes in the distance as Sage fights to keep up. He mutters, “I really hope we make it home before it begins to rain.”

She glances up at the sky casually and replies, “We have about a mile and a half remaining, and more thunder rumbles. A little rain isn’t going to hurt; it just gives us a reason to get home quicker.”

Just as she makes the statement, it starts drizzling.

“Great, of course, it’s raining,” he retorts sarcastically.

She takes off a little quicker, “C’mon, let’s go. You need to pick it up.”

The clouds open, and it starts pouring. He yells to her, “What! You're just going to leave me?”

She looks back at him and yells, “You're moving too slow, there ain’t no reason for us both to get soaking wet.” She turns around and breaks into a sprint.

The rain steadily descended, and he slowed almost to a walk. He starts jogging again with a slightly quicker pace. As he gets wetter, frustrated, he thinks, *Damn, this sucks.* He takes a deep breath and starts mumbling to himself to get motivated. *Let’s go, what doesn’t kill you makes you stronger*. He bends down and places his hands on his waist to catch his breath. The rain is drenching him.

Stephon is fixing an egg and cheese sandwich at home in the kitchen. He grabs a glass and pours himself some apple juice. He then takes a seat and looks at his tablet.

Sydney comes in through the back door, soaking wet from the rain. She enters the pantry, grabs a black bath towel, and begins drying herself.

“Where’s Sage?”

“Still jogging.”

“Are you going to pick him up?” He asks after taking a bite of the sandwich.

She quizzically looks at him, “No, why would I do that?”

He takes another bite, “Why would you go running when you knew it would rain?”

"I thought we could do it before it started to rain. You can't control the conditions you deal with, what's placed before you. This will toughen him up." She wipes down her legs and arms.

He sips his apple juice, "Do you believe you are being too hard on him?"

She feels disrespected by the question and loudly responds, "This is next level! He is going to be on a plane that very few people have ever been on. It is something we have never experienced before. Once he steps out as the Blac Angel, he will be a target for everybody. You are complaining more than he has."

Not impressed, he asks sharply. "Are you sure you're not doing this just for yourself, trying to relive a missed opportunity?

Sage suddenly comes through the front door, soaking wet as he drips rain on the doormat. They both look over at him. He's tired but happy to be out of the rain. He heads up the stairs.

"Wait! Come here. I want to ask you something?" She yells at him.

Sage complains, "I just want to shower and get out of these clothes."

She enters the pantry, retrieves a blue towel for him, and hands it to him. He begins wiping his arms.

She looks at him. "Do you think I'm too hard on you?"

He stops wiping and looks at her, “When we were in the backyard, and I changed into the Blac Angel for the first time, I felt so powerful. Like nothing I had ever felt in my life. I knew then I wanted it. If this is what I have to do to become him, then I'm down. I know her being hard on me is from a place of love, so I’m good.”

He opens and closes his hands to show off his hard work, making his veins in his forearms pop. He is proud of his new physique.

Stephon from the kitchen, “So, you ready to do this even if you might get killed?”

“Yeah. I don’t want to die, but if it’s for the right reason. This is my chance for redemption. I’ve done way too many bad things. Now is my chance to do good. While in the coma, I saw that this is bigger than me. I can make a change in the hood and maybe even the world.”

Impressed by the change in Sage’s heart, Stephon shakes his head approvingly, “You’re a grown man, and I‘m not going to interfere if this is what you want to do. I will do whatever I can to help.”

He returns the towel to his mother, “Can I shower now?”

“Yeah, go ahead. One more thing, we step it up more tomorrow.”

<<<<>>>>

Shady and Ciarra come into the trap house. Q and Amira are sitting on the couch, each on their phone. Ciarra goes and sits down beside Amira. At the same time, Q stands up and greets Shady.

“Damn, it’s pouring out there,” Shady complains.

He and Q exchange dap and the 187s handshake.

“Come here, let’s go talk in the room.” Q says. They walk into Q’s bedroom. In a calm tone, Q tells him, “I need you to take care of Big Saint. He stopped through last week. He ain’t 187 no more. He knows too much; we all go down if he snitches.”

Shady, surprised by the request, “You think he would turn on us?”

“That’s not the point! If he is going to be done with us, we gonna be done with him! We need to ensure he won’t be a problem later.”

Shady retorts, “Ever since he has been home, he has been on the down low. I never see him. Shady, still a little thrown by the order, “I thought Big Saint was your boy.”

“My boy? Ain’t nobody, my boy. Nothing or nobody is bigger than this! If you had done it right the first time, we wouldn't be talking now.”

“Yo, dawg, slow down! That’s on that crooked pig! We were just doing Kong, and that mission was a go. We had no idea Big Saint was with him. Now you want me to take care of him?”

“Yeah, nigga you deaf? Make it happen!” He gets up and walks out of the room.

TWENTYSEVEN

Sage sleeps deeply as Sydney, in her angelic form, enters his subconscious. She gently explains, "The next phase of your training takes place in this world." She then extends her right hand, which he grasps with his left, and together they are transported into a cylinder of light. Their journey ends in a vast, dark, starry void.

"What kind of training are we doing here?" He inquires.

Without responding, she extends her black wings and performs a full 360-degree spin, while the ancient Roman Colosseum begins to materialize around them.

Once finished, they hover about ten feet above the ground at the center. "What better place to test your skills than the original fighting arena?"

"Are we going to fight?"

"Battling is essential to the job, eventually, once you get familiar with your new powers. The training here will accelerate your transition to Blac Angel. You cannot be injured or hurt here, so we will use extreme methods to prepare you. Any questions?"

He shakes his head no.

"Let's get to it." She spreads her black wings out to their full glory and soars straight up into the dark sky.

Seventy feet in the air, she stops and hovers above him, “I need you to envision your wings so you can take flight.”

“How am I supposed to do that?”

“Focus, concentrate, see the wings forming.” She answers as she majestically levitates in the space void.

After a few seconds of him floating there without results, “I can’t do it.”

She flicks her right wing at him and outshoots a razor-sharp black feather that grazes across his left cheek. It lands on the dirt and fades away.

“What was that? he yells, shocked.

“That is a sharpened feather that’s in your bag of skills when you learn to formulate your wings. Now let’s go!” She flicks her right wing again, and two more razor feathers shoot out, landing inches from his feet.

“Okay, I can’t concentrate.” He complains.

She inhales deeply before gliding down smoothly. Carefully, she slides her arms under his armpits and lifts him with ease. Using a soft burst of strength, she rises to the top of the Colosseum, where the ancient stones tower below.

“Maybe this will help," she says softly, her voice tinged with anticipation as she rises higher, twirling gracefully to gather momentum before launching him into the vast, star-lit sky. He lets out a startled scream of terror and suddenly begins to plummet through the darkness. Out of nowhere, his wings unfurl dramatically, expanding about ten feet above the ground in a desperate attempt to catch him, but it's too late to prevent the inevitable crash. He lands face down with a heavy, echoing thud.

He gets up, surprised that he is not injured. Sydney swoops down beside him, "You did it, now you need to work on controlling them for flight! Let's try it from higher up to give you more time to work on that."

"That won't be necessary." He closes his eyes, and the majestic coal-black eight-foot-long wings form between his shoulder blades. Still with his eyes closed, they move slowly, flapping magnificently until he rises above the ground.

Her eyes sparkle with excitement as she takes his hand and gently lifts him, eager to let him practice flying around the grand Colosseum. They rehearse soaring straight up, gliding, swooping down, dive bombing, and hovering smoothly in midair, exploring different flight possibilities.

After thirty minutes, they go back to the arena. "You must learn to project your razor feathers." An archery target emerges roughly two hundred yards in the distance. She raises her hands in front of her.

"Your feathers can cut through metal and concrete, depending on how much force you use. You need to be careful and precise when sending them out."

She flips her left wing, then right, and two feathers zip out. They are traveling so fast that they are blurs. Both land in the center yellow bullseye and fade away quickly.

Sage shakes his head approvingly.

“Go ahead and take your shot.”

Seeing how easily she did it, he feels pretty confident.

He looks at her and retorts, “I got this.”

He flips his right wing, then left, and about twenty feathers shoot out in every direction. Seven feathers hit the target, and none landed in the bullseye. The rest fly off into dark space.

“I did not know you could throw a lot of them at once.”

That was a lesson for later. Power is meaningless without control. It’s all about mastering power, control, and timing. When you achieve all three, it becomes a beautiful thing. She flicks her left wing, and three feathers land perfectly in the center circle.

He smiles at her, “Now you're just showing off. Can I try again?”

“Go ahead. Take your time, and only shoot one. We need to master control.”

He steps forward directly in front of the target, carefully flicks his right wing, and, surprisingly, one feather shoots out and sticks to the top of the outer blue circle.

She flutters her wings as a sign of approval, "There you go, all you need is practice."

He does it again, and the feather lands almost in the exact spot.

"We can get back to it. You know how to shoot projectiles. Here's how to protect yourself against them."

She flies to the target and stands before it, "Shoot some feathers down and try to hit me."

He lines up in front of her and flips his wing, sending ten feathers toward her. She extends her left hand and waves it in front of the approaching feathers. They slow down to a tenth of their original speed. She then reaches out, catches one, and redirects it back toward Sage. Quickly, she flies back to him at super speed. She positions herself in front of him, shielding him with her right wing from the oncoming feather.

"What was that!?" You flew faster than the feather!" He exclaims, unable to contain his excitement.

"When you are in combat, every second counts. It's called 'Chronokenisis' or time manipulation. You have the power to slow down time for five seconds. This works on people and objects within twenty feet of you. This is a crucial ability. It can make the difference between living and dying."

"All you have to do is wave your hand, and you will project energies to slow down time. You can only do it in five-minute increments. Time needs to chance to reset itself. Trying to do it too much will alter time and reality."

"How were you able to fly so fast?"

"I actually teleported back. In extreme moments, you can teleport to a spot if you can see where you are going. This skill will have to be developed over time. I need you to focus on Chronokenisis.

She turns to the target and moves it fifty yards closer. She then sends him directly in front of it.

"This is close. Will I have enough time to do it?"

She ignores his question and answers, "You work better under pressure."

He floats above the ground and looks at her. He nods his head at her.

She quickly flips her left and then her right wings at him. He swiftly raises his right hand in front of him from right to left. Ten sharpened black feathers come directly at him. He quickly slides to his right. Four feathers slow down immediately, while the others are out of sync. The last six feathers fly into the area and slow for a brief moment. The moment freezes, and all the feathers hit the center. The feathers quickly dissipate in the target, and although he can't be injured, he's glad he didn't get hit. He barely makes it out of the target zone.

He floats back to her, and she tells him, "See. You are better under pressure."

“I want to practice more.”

“Not now, we need to get back to the world. After you and your father finish work, we will continue. The rest of your training will happen here.”

She grabs his hand, and they fly off.

TWENTYEIGHT

Over the past month, Sage has trained in the astral realm to become the Blac Angel. Sydney has repeatedly goaded, poked, insulted, and belittled him to prepare for future battles. In the colosseum, Sage floats three feet off the ground, surrounded by four Chinese Wing Chun dummies performing different hand strikes. His frustration grows from the constant training, as he feels he is prepared for real combat.

"This is boring. When am I going to become the Blac Angel?"

Sydney, levitating above, asks, "You believe you're ready?"

Not wanting to sound too boastful but feeling it, he enthusiastically shouts, "Let's go! Let's get it!" He begins executing different jiu-jitsu hand strikes and kicks at the Wing Chun dummies around him.

She looks down, unimpressed, and states, "Dummies don't hit back."

She softly descends and hovers approximately two feet above the ground. She waves her right hand, making the training dummies vanish.

He looks at her, "What do you have in mind?"

Sydney lands on the ground, and her wings disappear. She then spreads her arms out, filling the Colosseum with cheering spectators. She looks at him. "How will you do against an opponent that strikes back?" She takes a Wing Chun defensive stance.

"I can't hit you, you're my mother." He yells incredulously.

"In this world, I'm not your mother." She throws a straight left fist strike on his chest, knocking him twenty feet away. The crowds loudly cheer.

Stunned, he swiftly gets up and takes a front karate stance. She jumps at him and lands directly in front of him. He attempts a left straight punch that she blocks by grabbing his wrist. She slides to his left side, grabs his throat with her right hand, and throws him to the ground. He lands on his back, quickly gets to all fours, and kicks her in the stomach with his right foot, catching her off guard. He rolls over and promptly gets back to his feet. He then throws a right straight punch, which she blocks, making her forearms cross over like an X, then pushes his arm upwards, exposing his ribcage, which she thrusts with her right palm. This causes him to clutch his ribcage. She then forms the left wing and flicks it across his face, cutting him. The crowd cheers again. There are several scratches across the right side of his face. They quickly vanish. He complains, "You cheating you didn't say we could use our powers."

"There is no such thing in battle. Your foe will use anything to win. You must be willing to do the same."

He is angry now and charges at her aggressively. She spins to her left out of his way and then slams an elbow into the back of his neck. He falls to the ground and turns his leg counterclockwise, and sweeps her to the ground. He jumps up off the ground, and while in mid-air, his wings form, and he flips five feathers from his right wing at her. While on the ground, she waves her left hand, slows down the feathers, and rolls out of the way. Regular time returns, and the feathers hit the ground. He then performs a dive bomb toward her, hitting her in the chest and knocking her thirty feet back. She slyly smiles at him, impressed with his showing. He is doing better than she expected. She forms her wings and flies aggressively toward him. She slings her right wing towards him, throwing twenty sharpened feathers at him. Then does the same with her left wing. The feathers land and pin both his arms, spread-eagled on the ground. They hit with such force that they are embedded in the hard dirt, trapping him. Coming in at full speed, she is about to land on top of him, and he suddenly swings both his legs up and kicks her in the back, catching her off guard, causing her to crash land twenty feet away. Out of nowhere, the Supremacy appears, floating directly in front of Sage. The feathers trapping him vanish. He raises both arms above his head, and lightning shoots from his hands, making a thunderous sound that shakes the whole stadium.

"Enough!! This is over!" His voice is as booming as the thunder. "He has demonstrated he has the skills to hold his own against you. Now, only real-time experience can take him to the next level!"

Sage listening, asks, "Are you saying I'm ready to be the Blac Angel?"

"When you see me again, you will be the Blac Angel."

TWENTYNINE

Sage, Sydney, and Stephon are at the table finishing up dinner. Stephon looks at his son, "Tonight's the big night, huh?"

He takes a deep breath to conceal his excitement and says, "Yeah, I can't front I'm a little nervous."

Sydney, clearing the table, hears this and replies, "Nerves are good to keep you on edge."

"What time are you going out?" Stephon ask

"With this being the first time, you need to take it slow. We need to be careful, maybe go early and come back after about an hour or so until you get used to it." Sydney answers.

Sage gets up from the table, yawning, "I'm going to try and get some sleep."

"That's a good idea. I will wake you up in a few hours." Sydney tells him.

Stephon hears the bedroom door shut. He grabs Sydney by her hand as she wipes down the table. "Can you sit down? I want to ask you something, and be honest with me."

She stops and sits across from him, “I already know what you are going to ask. ‘Do I think he is ready?’

He nods his head in agreement. She answers, “He is getting there, but I’m not sure he’s there tonight. Since we started, I have seen significant growth in him. There is only so much training you can do; at some point, you must let them go. We have been saying it over and over: experience is the best teacher. Tonight, his experience begins. I will be with him, and we will take it slow.”

Stephon takes a deep breath and smiles at her, “All I can do is trust in you and the Lord.”

<<<<>>>>

Sage stands on the back porch, gazing at the eerily clear, star-filled night sky. His parents come quietly, but a tense, electric feeling fills the air. Sage clenches his fists, rubbing his hands with a combination of wild excitement and shadowed anticipation.

“Put this on.” She holds the Crusaders' cross in her left hand and gently places it around his neck.

Stephon watches intently, “You ready? Tonight is your world premiere.”

“I’ve been anticipating this moment ever since that first night I became Blac Angel.”

Stephon tells him, “Tonight is for real. Your life will change after this; you will lead two lives. You are going to make some people angry, and they will come after you.

You need to be careful and keep these lives apart. If they find out who you are…"

Sage looks over at him, worried he knows where this is going, "If something was to happen to y'all because of this, I don't know what I would do," he mutters quietly. Attempting to lighten the mood, he looks at Sydney. "Can we do this while I'm still young?"

Sydney rolls her eyes, "Patience, son, now repeat after me, Dum vivimus vivamus." He starts chanting, and the transformation begins.

He steadily grows taller and stronger, with his arms, legs, chest, and abs developing prominent muscles. As he enlarges, the cross begins to glow with a bright, flickering light that is blinding. The crystal jewels embedded within catch fire, erupting into fierce, dancing flames. Slowly, the bright glow diminishes, and his growth stops. This entire transformation takes less than thirty seconds, leaving him at 6'2 "tall with 50 pounds of lean, muscular bulk. He wears a sleek, tight-fitting black suit.

Stephon stares at him in disbelief at the transformation that has taken place. He gasped, "I would never have believed it if I didn't see it."

"I'll be right back." She abruptly leaves and jogs upstairs.

She returns with a black mask similar to what TV wrestlers wear.

"If you're going to be a superhero, you need to dress like one."

"Even with the physical change in your body, you still look the same. Here, put this mask on to help hide your face." She gives it to him.

Sage formulates his wings for the first time in the world. Stephon sees this and is totally blown away. He walks over, looks at his coal-black wings, sees the dagger-sharp feathers, carefully rubs one of them, and whispers, "This is incredible."

Sage warns him, "Be careful."

Sydney looks up, and she offers some last-minute advice, "Remember, you are just observing from above. If you see something happening, take care of it. Do not jump into anything bigger than you can handle."

Sage is very anxious now. "Okay, can I go now?" He asks impatiently.

"Wait, one more thing we need to pray." Stephon offers. They hold hands and make a small circle.

Stephon softly prays

The light of God surrounds us,

The love of God enfolds us,

The power of God protects us,

The presence of God watches over us,

Wherever we are, God is,

And where God is, all is well. Amen

She hugs him, “I will be joining you soon.”

Stephon looks at him and smiles, “I’m proud of you, son.”

They both retreat cautiously as he majestically unfurls his magnificent eight-foot wings. After a single powerful flap, he lifts off. With a swift second flap, he soars boldly into the dark, starry night sky.

Sydney goes to the shed in the back and takes a seat on the yoga mat. She gets into the lotus position, ready to mind-meld with him.

THIRTY

It is a calm, clear night, with the sky above him dotted with shimmering stars. The air feels significantly colder than what he has felt before in the astral realm, causing a shiver to run through his spine. Seeing the quiet darkness as an opportunity, he begins to practice flying. He pushes himself straight upward, cutting through the peaceful night to rise above the swirling clouds, aiming to stay hidden from the ground below. He intends to get more used to the sensation of flying in the natural, earthly world. As he gracefully swoops and glides through the fluffy clouds, he relishes the exhilarating feeling of movement and freedom. Suddenly, a gentle, reassuring voice whispers in his mind: Sage, I'm here. *Why are you so quiet?*

I didn't know what you were doing and didn't want to scare you.

I'm flying to get used to this world.

I'm glad you didn't rush into anything. Practice will make you a better Angel.

He practices several flight maneuvers for the next 20 minutes, including gliding, swooping, dive-bombing, and flying straight up.

I wonder how fast I can go? He asks.

Let's find out. She answers.

He leans sharply forward, tilting horizontally while flapping his wings forcefully. His speed exceeds expectations as he pushes ahead, with everything around him turning into a blur of motion. The cold wind bites his face, reminding him that goggles would help protect his eyes from the wind and debris.

Maybe you should slow down since you are still learning.

If you insist, he responds. He knew he hadn't reached his limit, but he was getting nervous.

He slows down. questions: *Where are we*?

I don't know. I'll separate to see where we are.

He turns around and goes below the clouds. *I don't know where I'm at, but I came from that direction.*

Blac Angel starts casually flying back, looking down at buildings, hoping to recognize something. He soon realizes that they all look the same from the sky.

Sydney has rejoined him. We are in Cedarwood, I saw the welcome sign there.

Lowkey, he is impressed that he could fly over 40 miles from home so quickly.

He flies back home just as fast.

Once returning to Elk City, he flies lower and notices 187th Street. Blac Angel looks down and recognizes the pimp from the night she and Kong made the pickup. The pimp shoves one of his tricks to the ground and yells at her.

"I got something I need to take care of, Blac Angel relays to Sydney.

He lands on the roof of Hotel 7 across the street. Sydney, surprised by this action, asked, "What are you doing?"

I'm bout to set this nigga straight about beating up on women.

He gradually descends from the roof into the hotel's parking lot. As he walks over to the pimp, his wings disappear. The pimp continues to shout at the woman on the street, while two other women watch in terror, hesitant to intervene.

"Hoe, don't talk back to me. You do what I tell you when I tell you!" He shoves her to the ground.

Be careful. Sydney relays to him. He ignores her. He is focusing on the pimp.

The pimp sees him coming across the street with his costume and mask and mockingly asks, "What's with the outfit, fool? Halloween still two months away. You think you're a superhero?"

Blac Angel helps the girl to her feet, but she is hesitant, confused by his outfit. She looks like a teenager, maybe sixteen or seventeen. She stumbles, struggling to shuffle away in her black high heels and red mini skirt.

He looks at the pimp and says, "Call me the Blac Angel If you want a superhero read a comic book, I'm real. You are done beating on women."

The pimp walks up to him, chewing on a toothpick, and snarkily answers, "You or nobody else is going to tell me what to do with my tricks!"

"Women are not property; you need to show them more respect. Without women, none of us would be here. No nation can succeed without its women. Your mother and sister are women. Do you disrespect them?"

"My momma ran out on me when I was four, so fuck her, and fuck you!" He throws a right cross that catches Blac Angel on his left jaw. His head moves slightly to the right. He looks at the pimp and smiles at him.

The pimp is shocked that the punch didn't affect him. He then throws a right hook to Blac Angel's gut, but he doesn't flinch.

Now the pimp is a combination of anger and amazement. He grabs a butterfly knife from his jeans' right pocket and flips it open.

Sydney relays, *Quit playing with him.*

Blac Angel does a right foot high kick to the pimp's face, causing the knife to fly out of his hand. He flies twenty feet in the air, and he lands about forty feet away on his ass.

Damn, I didn't know he would go that far. I need to work on control.

The pimp shifts slightly to his left and swiftly retrieves a 9mm pistol. Blac Angel leaps high into the air, and as the bullets are fired while he's airborne, they deflect harmlessly off his body. Though the gunfire causes him to flinch, it does not wound him. After six shots are fired, the magazine is exhausted. He lands about four feet away from the pimp, still lying in the street. He drops the gun, his hands trembling in fear.

Are you hurt? She asks nervously.

No, I'm good.

Blac Angel sarcastically says, "Only six rounds? What kind of pimp only has six rounds in these streets?" He stands over him, snatches the gun off the street, brings it up to his chest, and squeezes the barrel shut with both hands.

Blac Angel drops the gun back on his chest. "Here's a souvenir to help you remember me." He then bends down and, with his right hand, picks up the pimp. His wings appear, and he brings the right wing underneath the pimp's chin, with the sharp edge right at his Adam's apple. In a threatening tone, he sneers to the pimp, "Spread the word, Blac Angel is here. NO Women will be disrespected in these streets again! Next time I see you, you won't be so lucky." He causally tosses him into a broken-down car parked on the side of the street.

The pimp lying on the side of the road yells, "You are the one who won't be so lucky!"

Without responding, he gently takes off and floats away gracefully. He looks down and sees all three prostitutes videoing him with their phones.

Sydney relays to him *That was an interesting first night. You're about to go viral now. Let's go home.*

THIRTYONE

Stephon and Sage are in his truck, heading to a landscaping job. It's too early at seven in the morning to be doing this. Sage dozes in the passenger seat. Stephon is excited to hear about Sage's Blac Angel outing, asking, "How was being a superhero last night? I wanted to talk, but you got back so late I fell asleep."

Sage groggily responds, "It was fun."

The Rev excitedly answers, "Fun? That's all? You can fly and are probably stronger than anyone on Earth. That's the coolest thing ever."

A rush of energy overcomes him after hearing his father's excitement. "You're right. I was flying last night. I kicked a pimp's butt. I got shot, and I barely felt it."

Stephon, "Wait, hold it? You got shot? What happened?"

"I saw a pimp beating a woman, and it reminded me of your lessons to respect women and never hit them. Seeing him beat on her set me off. When I confronted him, he pulled his gun and shot me. The bullets bounced off; I barely felt them. I think I'm bulletproof!"

"You didn't feel the bullets at all?" Stephon asks in disbelief.

"They felt as if I was to get punched by Aiden."

Stephon, with a concerned look, asked," What type of gun was it?"

"I don't know a pistol. Why?"

"You could run into somebody with a bigger weapon that could be bad for you."

"Trust me, Dad, I'm good between the powers and mom in my head; everything's cool. You knew this could happen."

He sighs and states, "I want to talk with your mom about this."

Sage chuckles to himself and sighs. "Whatever."

They pull up to a huge multi-level white brick house with a front yard about the size of half a football field. The driveway circles up to the front door.

Stephon turns off the truck and looks at him. "We will finish this when we get home." He gets out and starts unloading the lawnmowers.

<<<<>>>>

Nine pm, and Blac Angel is flying above in the cool night air. He enjoys free flying. He relays to Sydney *Thank you for talking to Dad.*

He worries about you, and hearing that your son was shot is difficult. It's easier for him to accept because he knows I'm with you. If I were in his place, I would feel the same.

Sage answers, *he needs to understand that it's gonna get crazier if we do what we're trying to do.*

Blac Angel dives out of the clouds and heads toward his old spot on the corner. The same thing is still happening at the location. This is his first time at the spot since coming home. Now he is ready to send the message that Blac Angel is here.

Sydney tells him. *Let's see what's happening before we go rushing in blindly.* He lands on the rooftop of the convenience store and looks down at two hustlers from the 187s. They run up to cars at the stoplight. Most cars ignore them, but a few turn into the parking lot. Afterward, somebody runs to the car, does the deal, and keeps it moving. It usually takes less than a minute. He has seen it and done it hundreds of times; he is ready to make a difference in his hood. Blac Angel glides down to the corner. Trae, a youngster, steps to him. He has a black bandana around his neck. He looks Blac Angel up and down and, with a snarl, says, "What's with the costume? Who you supposed to be, my boy?"

Blac Angel answers with the same energy, "I'm shutting this corner down."

Trae pulls up his blue tank top and flashes his gun. "I don't think so, partna. You'd best take your costume-wearing ass out of here before you catch this fade." He then whistles for his boy on the corner, flagging down cars. He looks up from the car and starts to shuffle over.

His friend is coming over. We need to do something, Sydney tells him.

Trae pulls the gun out and points it at Blac Angel. He fires it at him. Blac Angel moved so swiftly to the left that he felt like his body was snatched. With his right hand, he grabs his right wrist, flips Trae to the ground, and snatches the gun. He hits the magazine release and drops it. The other banger sees this and runs up to Blac Angel from behind. He throws a right cross to the back of the head, causing him to stumble. Blac Angel quickly recovers from the blow, spins around to the banger's rear, and grabs his right wrist and elbow. With fierce precision, he delivers a powerful palm strike directly to the back of his elbow, causing it to snap painfully. The Banger screams in agony. Taking advantage of his suffering, he then clips him sharply with his foot, knocking him to the ground on his back. Unfurling his wings majestically, he stands over him slowly, drawing a sharp feather from his wing and pressing it threateningly under his throat. His voice is cold and commanding: "Don't get up." Trae is back on his feet, swings at Blac Angel, which he blocks with his right elbow, and throws a left jab into Trae's chin. Trae is stunned by this and backs up. He then kicks him with his right leg. Blac Angel blocks it with his left arm. His momentum spins Trae around, and with his right leg, he kicks down on the back of Trae's right knee, snapping it.

Trae yells out, "Aww shit, you broke my knee!" While still crouching, Blac Angel elbows him in the back of his head, causing Trae to fall face-first to the sidewalk, knocking him unconscious.

Sage, somebody is coming up behind you!

Suddenly Blac Angel falls to the ground. Another banger has hit him in the head from behind.

Blac Angel is getting pummeled from behind with a three-foot-long metal pipe.

His wings form and cover him, protecting him. *You can't cover up. You need to attack back. They are going to keep beating you.* Sydney tells him.

He rolls over onto his back. The attacker is another banger who just came out of the store. He is bigger and stronger than the other two. The cross on his chest begins to glow with a white light. Blac Angel doesn't know why. Blac Angel unfurls his wings fully and jumps to his feet. The banger swings the pipe at Blac Angel again, but this time he catches his wrist before the blow lands. The banger struggles to break free, but he cannot. Blac Angel, smiling now, squeezes his wrist, snapping bones and causing him to drop the pipe as his hand goes limp. The banger screams out in agonizing pain and looks at him in amazement because of his bone-crushing strength. He then yanks him up by his collar and floats ten feet above the ground, holding him above his head. The banger's feet are dangling above the street. He is too shocked to say anything. "*Now show them who's the boss*," Sydney relays to him. With the banger above his head, Black

Angel looks at him, smiles, and one-handedly body slams him onto the concrete. The banger's wind is knocked out of him, and he struggles to catch his breath.

Police sirens are blaring in the distance. He knows he's got to leave. He leans down on the banger's chest as he struggles to breathe, holding his broken right wrist, "Tell Q the 187s days are coming to an end." He flies straight up in the night sky.

THIRTYTWO

Stephon sits at the table with his tablet, reviewing today's sermon. Sage comes down the stairs, feeling sore but pretty good. He takes a seat across from his dad. Stephon sets his tablet aside and looks at Sage, saying jokingly, "Good morning, son, or is it, Blac Angel?"

Chuckling at the quip, he answers, "Sage works."

Stephon picks the tablet back up, "I was checking out the news this morning, and Blac Angel is all over the web. You're famous."

He slides the tablet over to Sage, who then picks it up. The screen displays a clip of him fighting at the convenience store, followed by another of him kicking the pimp into the air. A few clips also show people claiming it is fake, using tricks, cameras, and special effects. Sage mutters, "Everybody's got a camera."

"You've been the Blac Angel for less than a week and gone viral," Stephon replies.

Inside, Sage is thrilled about the attention Blac Angel is receiving.

Sitting there tapping his finger on the table, thinking, "Would you be okay with Blac Angel speaking at church today?"

Surprised by the request, he answers, "What do you want to say?"

"To let the people know I'm real and here to help." He gets up from the table, "I'll see you at church."

At the service, Pastor Reed stands at the podium and looks at the congregation, "Before I get into today's sermon, we have a special guest who wants to speak to you. By now, I'm sure you have seen some videos of this young man doing incredible things. He is making a difference in our neighborhood, city, and, soon, the world. He has a message he wants to share with us today. I would like for you all to meet the Blac Angel."

Blac Angel glides in from the rear of the church without saying anything. He floats about one foot off the floor. His wings are out. Everyone in the church turns around. There is a gasp as people look around. For most of the congregation, this is the first time seeing him live. Some are clapping, while others are watching in wide-eyed awe. Everybody who has a phone start recording him. He floats up the four stairs and gently lands on the floor. His wings slowly disappear, prompting a loud gasp.

He nods his head to the Rev, who repeats the gesture. Blac Angel does not want to give any indication that they are related.

He leans into the microphone and says, "Good morning, church. I'm the Blac Angel. Today, I want to address some of the social media rumors about me. There's a lot of fake and false information out there, but I'm here to tell you I am real. What you've seen is not fake or filtered. God grants my abilities. I will use my gifts to clean up Elk City and clear out the gangs that have taken control."

After this announcement, everybody in the church immediately stands up and gives him a standing ovation, whooping and hollering. After about a minute, he motions for them to settle down with his hands.

He continues, shouting, motivated by the crowd, "To kill a snake, you need to cut off the head, and the head of the snake is the 187's! I'm giving them one week to shut down, or I will take them out. I will put down every gang that follows. This is a war we can't afford to lose. Once the gangs are dealt with, we will keep the streets safe. This is not a threat, this is my promise! What's understood doesn't need to be discussed. Thank you, and God Bless everybody."

Again, he receives another standing ovation from the congregation. A wide grin forms on his face. He is enjoying every minute and soaking in the applause.

His wings form, and he rises off the floor. Ten feet into the air.

Questions are being yelled at him, "Who are you?" Where did you come from? What kind of powers do you have? God gave you powers. Why you?"

Blac Angel ignores the questions, floats down the aisle, and leaves the church.

Amira's in the congregation, recording the whole thing. She quickly texts Q: "*You need to watch this video.*"

THIRTYTHREE

The church service has ended, and everyone is socializing about the Blac Angel speech.

Amira and Aiden are walking down the crowded aisle when she sees Sage in the back pew, waiting patiently to get out. They stop and wait for him.

Amira, “I didn’t think you were here today. You usually sit with your family.”

“I got here late. I wasn’t feeling too well earlier,” Sage replies.

Sage knows Aiden saw Blac Angel today and is curious about his impression of him.

“What did you think of Blac Angel?”

“He can fly. He’s cool.” Aiden quickly answers.

Amira looks at Sage, “What did you think?”

“Hopefully, he’s a man of his word and does what he says he will do.”

“Bro, how you going to be like that? Q and the 187 treated you like family.” She states incredulously.

“Do families kill each other? Q ain’t nothing but a wolf in sheep's clothing. He’s the reason Kong is dead. He fools people with the slick, smooth facade. He's a user and bully who only keeps people around for what they can do for him; you, of all people, know this."

Amira hears the spite in his tone and retorts, "I know he took me in when no one else would, including you."

"Be real now; you know my family ain't gonna let my baby mama stay up in their house unless we married, and we both know that ain't happening." He shakes his head as he talks.

"Whatever, I know this Blac Angel is gonna be trouble."

Sage answers, "That depends on your point of view."

Frustrated with the conversation, she storms away. "I'll pick up Aiden later today."

Amira's in her car, leaving the church, and she calls Q. He groggily answers, *"What's good?"*

"Did you watch that video?" She inquires.

Annoyed, he answers, *"What video?"*

"That man, the superhero, Blac Angel, showed up at church today and gave a speech. He told everybody he is shutting the 187s down."

After hearing this, Q sits up in his bed. *"Am I supposed to be nervous, scared? I don't care who he is or what he says. Can't know one man shut us down. Chill out."*

"You need to watch that clip; that's all I'm sayin." She hangs up.

He looks at his phone and checks out the video. As he watches it, he glares at the screen, his breathing is getting heavier and heavier, and he's seething inside. Every word Blac Angel speaks gets him angrier.

After the video, he mutters, "I got one week homey?? Well, you got less time than that. Let the countdown begin."

He texts Shady. "Get the war council together."

Q and Shady are in his suburban on the way to Francisco's Auto Repair. It is on the other side of Elk City, away from the 187's operation. Q pulls into the parking lot. The shop is an old gray concrete building with four large garage doors. They both get out, and Shady knocks on the front door. A tall Hispanic man in his thirties with a ponytail lets them in. They quickly dap each other up and walk to the garage. There are no cars in the garage. Five other men are sitting in a semi-circle on folding steel chairs, drinking forties. They each represent their sets. Nuke is with the Deceptors. Pedro is part of the Bloody Coyotes. Rachad the Dreadlocks. Last are Sanchez and Francisco, who are both with El Serpienete. Francisco quickly grabs two more chairs for Q and Shady. Q takes the chair but does not sit down, while Shady does. Q walks to the center of the circle and paces around inside it.

He stops and loudly announces, "We have a problem. By now, you all have seen those videos about this so-called Blac Angel saying he's gonna take us down in a week.

The way I see it, it gives us less than a week to do him. If your enemy tells you when he's going to strike, you strike first."

'Nuke,' a member of the Deceptors, responds, "Not us, homey you."

Thrown by the statement, Q steps to him, "You in business only because I allow you to stay." He spreads his arms apart and spins around the circle, "This all falls apart if I go down."

"Or maybe it's one hurdle removed that is keeping us from the top," Nuke yells back at him.

Q, upset with the continuous insubordination, steps over to Nuke and snatches him up by his gray t-shirt off the chair, causing it to fall. Nuke, with his right hand, reaches for the gun in his waistband. Q grabs his wrist and holds it down before he can pull out his piece. Francisco and Sanchez jump up, grab Q, and struggle pulling him away from Nuke. Nuke pulls out his weapon as they drag Q away. Shady jumps up, pulls his piece, and aims it directly at Nuke's head. Screams to him, "You don't want to do that, fool!"

The only one still sitting down, Pedro yells, "Whoa! Whoa! Bring it down! This ain't what we came to do! We got bigger thangs to deal with! The Blac Angel, y'all playin right into his hand! Get this shit worked out later. 'The enemy of my enemy makes you my ally.'

Q hears this, pauses for a second, and pushes him away, both Francisco and Sanchez, "Good point." He glances at Nuke while sliding his weapon back into his waistband, "Me and you got some unfinished business to take care of later."

Everybody goes and sits back down.

Francisco gets up and goes to the center, "What do we know about this dude?"

Rashad, still sitting down, yells, "The first time I saw a video, my boy Fresh got his ass beat by him. Fresh had to go to the hospital. I saw him a few days later, and he told me about it. The stuff he was telling me about Blac Angel, I thought he was hitting the pipe or something. Then I saw some of the videos and thought they were fake; most of that shit is fake. Fresh showed me the gun he crushed."

Francisco stands up, puts his right leg on the chair, and elaborates, "Okay, we know he is really strong and can fly. Humph, we need some serious weapons. The cops have some stuff that should take care of him."

Nuke excitedly asks, "What? We're supposed to break into a police station?"

"Relax, homey, I was throwing out ideas," Francisco states as he glares at him.

Shady, quiet throughout, reflects on Francisco's statement, saying, "I have something; my old reserve unit has whatever we need to take care of him."

Nuke sarcastically replies, "First, we talk about the police. Now a military base. Come on, partner, be real?"

Shady stands up, looks at Nuke, and states louder, "It's the National Guard, not a full-on military base. I was assigned there. I know the layout, and I know what they got."

Q's interest is piqued, "You think we could do this?"

"It's not always guarded, just a fence, alarms, and cameras. If we plan it right, we should be able to do it in maybe an hour."

"In that video he posted, he says we got a week, so we need to do this in five days. You think you can come up with a plan before then?" Q asks.

Shady looks around the shop at the various mechanical tools, "I should be able to if Fran lets us use some of his resources and if we get the manpower."

"No problem, partner. Whatever you need," They fist bump.

"Alright, gentleman, go back to your sets. Let them know what's up. We will be in contact. Operation Blac Angel Down begins."

THIRTYFOUR

The Blac Angel has been flying around Elk City for the last three hours and has not seen anything happening anywhere.

I'm heading home. Ain't nothing going on tonight. Sage relays to his mother.

Okay, I will see you at the house.

He flies home, lands in the backyard, and transitions back into Sage. As he walks in the back door, Sydney is already at the kitchen table with a bottle of water. He sits across from her. "What do you think is going on? Ever since Blac Angel gave that speech at church, it has been quiet. Do you think it scared them?"

She sips and shrugs her shoulder, "I guess that's possible, or what is more likely, is this is the calm before the storm."

"That means I have to stay on top of my game. I want to train later. I'm going to sleep. Goodnight."

"Whenever you are ready, I will meet you on the other side. Goodnight."

Francisco's garage the following night, around ten pm, with twenty to thirty bangers from their different sets present. They form a large circle, with Q and Shady standing at the center. Q spins around and shouts.

"Yo, everybody shut up! We have business we need to take care of. We have three days before this punk Blac Angel is supposed to take us down. My boy Shady has devised a plan to get us some firepower!"

He looks over at Shady, "It goes down tonight."

Shady paces around the circle aggressively, "Aight fools, we will load up and head to the Guard. Venom, Chase, and Tone will keep Blac Angel busy. For this to work, we must have perfect timing. Aight, let's do this." Francisco opens the garage bay doors, and everybody disperses to their vehicles.

Tone, Venom, and Chase jump into a white Lincoln town car and speed away.

Tone is in the driver's seat, with Venom in the passenger and Chase in the back. Tone takes a swig of the forty in the car, "Alright, fellas, we chillin until Shady tells us they are in place." He parks across the street from an all-night gas station.

Chase fires up a joint in the back, "Yo fools, y'all realize we're the crash dummies in this deal, right?"

"If we can take this fool down and get shit back to normal, it will be worth it," Venom states.

"As long as we don't get killed doing it." Tone adds.

Shady, Q, and three other bangers are in Q's Black Suburban. Behind them is a dark blue minivan with four more bangers. Bringing up the rear are Francisco and Sanchez in their company truck. They all park at a closed Pawnshop, and across the highway is the front gate to the Elk City National Guard.

"You sure there is no one guarding it?" Q asks.

On his phone, texting, Shady answers Q, "Yeah. The unit is out training for the next month."

He groups text to convey, "Be frosty."

Stephon and Sydney are sitting on the couch watching TV. Sage comes downstairs and tells them, "I think I'm taking the night off, you know, a chance to relax and recharge."

Stephon looks at him. "That sounds like a good idea."

"Are you sure? You don't want to go out for an hour. If nothing's happening, we can come home," Sydney replies to him.

A frown forms on Stephon's face as he looks at her, "It's okay if he takes a night off. It's not like he doesn't deserve it."

Sydney protests, “It’s just an hour. If nothing happens, we come back home. How would you feel if you didn’t go out and someone got injured or killed?”

Stephon yells at her, “Don’t do that! Don’t guilt-trip him into it! He could be the one killed or injured!”

Sydney looks at Sage, “I don’t understand when we first started. You were so excited about it. Now you don’t want to do it anymore?”

“It’s cool. I can do it for an hour. Let me go get the cross.”

After he leaves, Stephon looks at her and mumbles, “I know I said this before, but are you sure you are not trying to recapture some past chance?”

She stares hard at him, doesn’t respond, and walks to the kitchen.

<<<<>>>>

Tone Chase and Venom are still parked across the street from the gas station. Venom gets a text from Shady*: We set. Hit me back when it’s going down.*

He sits up in the back seat and puts his phone back in his jacket. “We're up.”

They all straighten up and look at the gas station. Tone takes the final swig of the forty. After ten minutes of sitting there and watching. A black-rimmed red Charger turns into the gas station. Tone starts the car, “That’s the one.” Chase and Venom pull the stocking caps over their face as the Charger stops at the pump. Tone quickly drives the Lincoln directly in front of the Charger.

Tone grabs his piece from the side door pocket and rushes towards the male driver, who is distracted by his phone and unaware of their approach. Venom and Tone exit the car and approach quickly. Venom enters the front passenger seat, while Tone tries to open the back door, but it's locked. He pulls on the handle in a frantic attempt to open it. Noticing this, Venom presses the unlock button. Meanwhile, Chase, aiming his gun at the man, yells, 'Put the key on the dashboard and get the hell out."

"Aight, just don't shoot me!" he exclaims as he swiftly takes the key fob from the center cup holder and carefully places it on the dashboard. Suddenly, Tone's grip tightens on him, yanking him forcefully out of the car. The man stumbles and crashes into the full trash cans near the gas pumps. Chase calmly steps over him without hesitation, slides into the driver's seat of the car, and speeds off into the night.

Venom texts, *We got a ride.*

Chase speeds down the road.

Venom gets a text back. *Keep your foot on the gas and stick to the route. Keep me posted.*

Shady tells Q, "They got a ride. Now we need Blac Angel to take the bait."

Growing impatient, Q asked, "How long do we have to sit here?"

"Homey, if this is gonna work, we need patience. When Blac Angel makes his move, then we make ours. Trust me. I got this."

"Aight, bro, I trust you." He fists bumps Shady.

Chase is barreling down the road, hitting up to one hundred miles an hour. He is running red lights on the way to the freeway. Tone and Venom have their windows down, with their heads out the window, looking out for Blac Angel. There are now three police cars with their sirens on, pursuing them.

Blac Angel flying above from a distance, see the police chasing the Charger. *That looks interesting.* He heads toward the pursuit.

Now, aren't you glad you came out tonight? You would have missed this. She relays to him.

Now is not a good time. The chase is on the service road, speeding toward the highway. The cops are still two or three car lengths behind. Blac Angel flaps harder to catch up with them as he gets closer. He slowly descends on them from above.

As he approaches the car, Sydney asks, *What's your plan?*

I don't know, maybe flip the car over.

If you do it at that speed, you will kill them.

In the back seat, Tone shouts urgently, “He’s back there!” as he leans out the rear window. Without hesitation, he pulls out a Mac-10 and starts firing wildly at Black Angel, with gunfire echoing through the air as rounds zip past, narrowly missing him. Blac Angel soars higher to get out of range. *I’ll catch them down the road.*

Venom quickly calls Shady and yells, “He is here, dawg, he is about to catch up with us!”

Shady hears the background noise, “Yo, do whatever you have to do to keep him busy!” He hangs up.

Q starts up his vehicle and excitedly yells, “It’s go time!” The three bangers in the back wake up from his excitement.

He drives over and gets on the two-lane road with the other vehicles following behind him. Q goes about five hundred yards to the turnaround spot. Shady turns to the bangers in the back, “There is a camera on the guard shack. Tape up the lens. Then come back and get the saw to cut the lock to the gate. Make sure to keep your face covered.”

Q turns onto a two-lane road. About two hundred yards away is an empty guard post. They stop, and the three bangers get out. They sneak up to the guard shack, and two bangers stand on the other's shoulder as he puts black tape on the camera. The third banger is the lookout. They sneak around the empty shack and do it to the other three cameras. They quickly jog back to the vehicle.

The taller one answers, “We're good,” as they jump in the vehicle.

“Alright, let’s go up to the gate.” Q drives and stops. Shady leans out the window and looks back. He yells to Francisco and Sanchez. “Get up here!”

They move into the left-hand lane, pass the minivan, and park next to Q. They pull their black masks over their faces, jump out of the truck, grab two cordless circular metal-cutting saws, and begin cutting the gates' metal clasp.

<<<<>>>>

Blac Angel lands about 75 yards in front of the Charger. It speeds toward him on the darkened service road.

You do know they aren’t going to stop? Sydney message.

Chase spots him in the middle of the street, his jaw clenched and eyes blazing with fury. His grip on the steering wheel tightens as he slams the pedal to the ground, voice trembling with rage as he mutters through clenched teeth, “I’m going to run this fool over.”

Blac Angel sees the car hurtling towards him. *I guess here’s the chance to test my time manipulation.*

Chase screams, “Shoot that motherfucker!” Venom yells back, “I can’t. I’m out.”

Twenty yards away, Blac Angel can see their faces, *Not yet, Not Yet... Not Yet...Sydney tells him.* Five yards away, she screams *NOW!!* He waves his right hand in front of them, slowing the car down to a tenth of the speed they were doing. Blac Angel levitates thirty feet over the car, spins around, and flicks both his wings downward, puncturing both rear tires with his sharpened feathers. This causes both back tires to burst. Chase refuses to stop and floors the gas pedal. Shredded rubber is flying everywhere, as sparks spit out from the rims, scraping the streets.

Venom yells, “What the hell are you doing? We can’t outrun them with two flats!” Chase yells back, “That MF Blac Angel gonna have to come get me.” Tone, hearing this, looks over at him with a scared expression, “I ain’t going out like this!” He suddenly opens the passenger door and rolls out of the car. A cop car sees this and quickly pulls up to surround him. The back rims are mangled; they are no longer round but oblong, forcing the car to slow down to a point where the cops overtake it. The first car comes up beside them on the left, forces them off the road into the grass, and stops in front of them, blocking their path. The second car approaches from the back and follows them into the field. Blac Angel lands on the car's roof and, with his right wing, makes a diagonal cut into it, followed by the same with his left wing, creating a giant X across it. He then rips it open. Seeing this, Venom jumps out of the car and runs toward the woods. Blac Angel bends down, yanks Chase up by the back of his shirt, and holds him above his head. Chase pleads, “Please don’t kill me!”

“Don’t worry, maybe next time,” he smirks confidently. Black Angel then casually hurls him at Venom, who is struck with such force that they both crash onto the ground in a tangle mess of limbs.

Two police officers run up to Chase and Venom, gets them on their feet, and place them in cuffs.

Three police officer are now pointing their gun at Blac Angel, “Am I under arrest too?”

One of the officers says, "If we had an encounter with you, we were instructed to bring you in for questioning.”

Blac Angel sees more cops slowly circling him, all with their weapons out. “What for? I am trying to help you clean up the streets and get rid of the gangs. We are all on the same side, we just have different ways of doing it.”

We are not going to the police station, I’m about to stun them. Sydney relays to him.

I had no plans on going with the cops. The cross erupts with a blindingly bright white light that slices through the darkness, intense and almost unbearable. All five police officers drop their guns and fall to their knees, instinctively covering their eyes to shield themselves from the overwhelming glare. Black Angel's wings emerge, spreading wide as he soars upward, vanishing into the night sky.

Francisco and Sanchez have cut a hole in the fence just big enough for them to drive through. On the base are several beige buildings that all look the same. Q leads the convoy while Francisco and Sanchez follow behind, with the minivan bringing up the rear. "Which way to the guns?" Q asks.

"The arms room is located in the headquarters building straight ahead. When you get there, park in the rear." They park in front of two garage doors.

Everyone exits their vehicles. They are all dressed in black tactical gear and wearing black face masks. Sanchez and Francisco grab the cordless saw and protective helmets, turn on their flashlights, and begin cutting the garage door.

Everyone else gathers around, waiting impatiently as they cut the metal door.

"What's the setup inside?" Q asks.

"It has an open bay area used for formations and vehicle maintenance. Then we have to go to the commander's office, where we can access the arms room. There is a side door from the commander's office to the arms room."

After fifteen minutes, they finally cut through the doors.

Shady turns around and yells to one of the gangbangers, "Go get the battering ram." The banger in the rear runs to the minivan, pops the hatch, and grabs the door battering ram.

"Let's move! Let's move!" Shady shouts.

They enter through the hole in the garage door. On the back wall of the landing, six steps lead to another door.

Shady loudly instructs, "Go up the stairs and bust it down."

The banger with the battering ram moves to the front of the line. He runs up the stairs, positions himself to the left, and swings the ram at the doorknob. After five swings, the door breaks at the knob, and the banger behind him kicks the rest of in. Shady steps forward, pulls out his cell phone, turns on the flashlight, and heads left down the hallway. The other bangers notice and follow suit. As they walk, their flashlights illuminate the hallway. They pass a heavy, brown, double-hung door split horizontally about twenty feet away. Shady shines his light on it and says, "That's the arms room."

They continue down the hall and pass another office. That door reads *First Sargent Thurston.*

Shady stops at the last door, "This is the captain's office. Knock it down." The same banger with the rammer comes in and slams into the door three times. After the third strike, it caves in. They quickly run into the office, and behind the Captain's desk to the left is another door.

"Damn, Shady, how many doors we gonna have to go through?" Q gripes.

Shady shines his light on Q's face. "Come on, bro. You put in the time. We ain't going after no toy guns here."

This metal door features a deadbolt lock with a handle positioned below the keyway. A metal plate shields the strike plate, reinforcing the area around the handle. The banger starts swinging with greater force than before. The rammer hits the metal plate and bounces back. It's unclear whether he's making any progress. After ten swings, he drops the rammer from exhaustion.

Not saying to anyone in particular, “I'm done, dawg.” He crouches down with his hands on his knees. Sweat has formed on his forehead.

Shady puts his flashlight in his cargo pants, grabs the rammer, and starts wailing away furiously at the plate after the seventh hit. The door pops open.

They all quickly run down a long, slim hallway. At the end of the hallway is another door. This door has a heavy metal sliding clasp securing it. Now in the front, Francisco slides the pin and opens the door.

He steps into the dimly lit room, shining his flashlight brightly to illuminate the surroundings. Following closely behind, their flashlights sweep across the space, searching intently. Lining the walls are empty green metal weapon racks that hold twenty M-16 rifles stacked vertically. There are approximately twenty of these racks dispersed throughout the room. All empty.

Q looks around the room, stunned, and shouts at Shady, “Where are all the damn M16's, SAWs, anything!”

"I told you the unit was deployed. I guess they took everything." Shady shouts, surprised as well.

"I found something," Francisco yells, standing to the right of the door they entered. He shines his light on two metal gun racks, each holding 20 weapons, stacked one above the other.

Everybody walks over to check it out. There are two full racks of M16's.

Q looks over at Shady, disgustedly yells, "We went through all this for twenty 16's? You disappointed me, dog. You got to put in some work to fix this. He turns around and walks away, yelling, "Let's grab them and get the hell out of here!"

THIRTYFIVE

Sage wraps up Wednesday night's choir practice, walking off the choir stand as most members head home for the evening. Aiden is peacefully sleeping in the first pew, while Sage quietly sits next to him to check his phone. Amira has sent a message saying, "On my way to get Aiden, will be there in a few."

The text was sent twenty minutes ago. He texts back *at choir practice.*

He switches up to text Candace. *Putting in work at choir practice, my reintroduction to singing is this Sunday. I hope you can make it.* He places his phone down.

Stephon enters the sanctuary and takes a seat beside him.

"You sounded good tonight, son, like you never left."

Amira discreetly opens the church doors, hears them talking, and stops. She kneels down so she can't be seen and leans in to eavesdrop.

Stephon looks over at Sage with concerned questions, "You think you can do both sing and be Blac Angel?"

Hearing this, Amira snaps her head back, and her eyes widen in shock and disbelief. Her mind races to process what she's just heard, struggling to grasp the reality of

Sage potentially being the Blac *Angel? How? Blac Angel is so much bigger and stronger. When did it happen?* She shakes her head, still in disbelief.

"I should be able to. They are two separate things with no connections."

"If this singing takes off. You never know."

Sage laughs, "That would be the best type of problem to have."

Stephon takes a deep sigh looks at him worriedly, "That deadline is coming up in a few days. You ready?"

Amira leans in closer, still ear hustling, *"Damn, Sage is Blac Angel. I knew something was different bout him, but never could have guessed this. It kinda makes sense. He comes home, then a few weeks later, Blac Angel shows up out of nowhere. How does he change to Blac Angel?*

Sage looks back at him, his brow furrowed with concern, "Blac Angel put it out. I don't have a choice."

Amira has heard enough. She yells out, "Sage! Sage! You here?" She walks into the church, down the center aisle to them. Stephon looks at her as she approaches, stands up, and tells Sage, "I will see you at home." He walks away up to the altar.

She sits down next to Aiden, who is still asleep.

"Choir practice, huh?"

He answers, "Yeah, I think I will sing with them this Sunday."

"Happy to see you get back to your normal life." She shakes Aiden's leg to wake him up. "I need to get him to his maw maw house." Aiden wakes up sleepily and stands up. He groggily follows behind her.

Sage yells, "Goodnight," as they leave.

He rechecks his phone. Candace has sent him a video smiling from her living room. She yells happily, "I can do better than Sunday. I'm back in town. We can do brunch tomorrow if you are free, and afterward. We can discuss your singing again. Let me know something."

He texts. *Whatever brunch works for me. I'll get back to you when I get home.*

<<<<>>>>

Amira is in the parking lot, excitedly texting Q. *Sage is Blac Angel.* She starts her car and begins to back out when her phone rings.

She already knows who it is as she answers through the car's Bluetooth, "Sage is Blac Angel!? What the hell are you talking about?" Q screams at her.

Turning out of the church parking lot, she replies, "I heard him and his father talking in church tonight."

"How!?" Q repeats.

"How the hell would I know! Bro, think about it. Blac Angel doesn't show up until after Sage comes home from the hospital. Then he drops out of the 187's. Now Blac Angel's coming after you. Do you think this is a coincidence? It all lines up."

"This Blac Angel fool is about four or five inches taller and jacked up. Sage is a weak punk. How's he doing it?"

She is tired of him repeatedly asking the same question in an irritated tone, and replies, "I don't know. He says being in that coma changed him. I guess this is what he is talking about."

Q, driving home, mumbles, "Shit, don't add up. Later." He hangs up.

He then quickly calls Shady. Who is at the gym working out on the bench. He is pushing over 3 bills on the bench without a spotter. He places the bar on the rack, sits up, and answers from his AirPods. Breathing heavily, "What's up?"

"We have the final war council tonight at Francisco at ten. I need you to be there as we go over last-minute details."

"I'm there. Just finishing my workout." He taps the pod to hang up.

<<<<>>>>

A mixture of anger and power rushes through Q and roars like a lion. "His deadline for us is Sunday! On this set, Blac Angel dies tomorrow night!"

They are meeting at Francisco's Garage, once again, and he's in the center of the circle, surrounded by twenty-five bangers.

"We stage here tomorrow at ten, strap up, then roll out. If you want to punk out, now is the time."

Everybody looks around at each other. Nobody leaves.

He speaks again, "Bet, Bet. We need to lure him into the trap. I got some inside info earlier tonight that will help with that. Once there, we give him everything we've got! Then no more so-called Black Angel!"

"What's the info?" Francisco asks.

"You'll find out tomorrow."

Nuke, twirling a toothpick in his mouth, steps from the back, "Then what?"

"What do you mean? 'Then what?" Q squares up to him and asks with a hint of anger.

"What happens after Blac Angel is gone?"

"Everything goes back to the status quo."

Twirling the toothpick in his mouth, he mumbles, "Or maybe there will be a new status quo."

Shaking his head and glaring at Nuke, his voice lowers, "Aight, cuz me and you can take care of this when this is done. He looks around, "If there is nothing else, we can all be out."

<<<<>>>>

The following morning. It's been raining overnight, so Sage and Stephon cannot work. Boredom and the upcoming battle inspire him to get a workout in. He goes to the shed and gets on the treadmill for cardio. After an hour of running, the weight of the battle is still on his mind. He decides to find his calm. He lights a few of the candles his mother has around the room, then turns off the light and sits in the lotus position as he drifts into a state of relaxation. Going deeper, he is drifting into the astral plane. This is his first time going there alone. As he drifts his entity, is guided to the temple to meet the Supremacy.

He is seated on the throne wearing the same outfit as before, the long black monk's robe with a hood over his face. He bellows, "I sense that you are troubled about your upcoming battle, and you seek words of comfort."

Sage is floating at the bottom of the altar. "Yes. I know I am doing the right thing. I am not comfortable with the possibility of innocent people being hurt."

'Uneasy is the head that wears the crown.' By accepting the mantle of the Blac Angel, you must also take on all the responsibilities that come with the power. Any life-altering situation carries residual effects. You have chosen this path, and I cannot step in. If you have prepared yourself and believe in what you are doing, that is all that can be expected. Do you still believe in what you are doing?"

"Yes, I do."

"Then go forward with a clear spirit and heart. Return to your world. Continue to prepare yourself."

He dismissively waves his right hand at and his entity instantly returns to his body. Once back in his physical body, he awakens to see his mother in the same lotus position to the left.

Sage does not disturb her, he stands up and prepares to leave when she speaks to him.

"Is everything alright?"

"Yeah, I was trying to find some peace, and the next thing I know, I was in front of the Supremacy. He spoke to me about the burden of being the Blac Angel."

She stands up and turns on the light. She asks excitedly, "You went to the astral plane without trying? Your gifts are developing. I came here to tell you that your father has a doctor's appointment today, and I'm going with him. You got any plans?"

They leave the shed and go inside, and stop in the kitchen. He goes to the fridge to get some juice she continues walking.

"I'm meeting up with Candace for some brunch later today." He tells her as he goes to the couch.

At the top of the stairs, she yells to him, "Have you asked her out yet?"

He lies on the couch and yells back to her, "Yes, but she is weighing her options, but I'm still working on it."

"Keep at it. I like her."

He pulls out his phone and texts *Candace, What time we doing brunch?*

She texts back *I will pick you up at your house at one.*

Cool. He texts back

He puts his phone on his chest and closes his eyes.

Ten minutes later, his phone buzzes on his chest. He believes it's another text from Candace.

He turns it over, and it's a video from Q,

The video is a close-up of him leaning on the front hood of his Suburban. He is dressed in all-black tactical gear.

"Big Saint!! What's up, you weak-ass nigga. Or is it, Blac Angel!? If you got the balls, be at your punk ass daddy's church in thirty minutes; it won't be there in thirty-one. Check this out."

He moves around to the rear of his suburban, opens the back hatch, revealing a variety of grenades neatly arranged inside. In the background, he observes a group of other bangers dressed in all-black tactical gear, armed with AR-15 rifles, standing alert and ready.

The video shifts back to Q, and with disdain in his voice, he continues, "Aight, Big Saint or Blac Angel or whatever your bitch ass is, be here in thirty." The video abruptly ends.

In a panic state, Sage jumps off the couch, runs up the stairs, and grabs the Crusaders' cross from his dresser.

He calls his mother, who answers from the car as they arrive and park for the appointment.

Before she says anything, he yells, "Q knows I'm the Blac Angel!"

"What? How?" She stammers incredulously.

"I don't know! He just sent a video saying he'll blow up the church if I don't show up in 30 minutes. He called me Blac Angel."

Stephon listens, "He's talking about blowing up my church!! What kind of sick man would blow up a church?"

She starts the car and backs out of the parking spot.

In a stern voice, she warns Sage, "Don't do anything until we get back home. We should be there in less than thirty."

"If you are not back, I'm doing what I got to. I will not let them blow up Dad's church."

She yells at him, "Don't do nothing without me!" He hangs up on her.

He paces nervously in his room, feeling scared and anxious, with a knot in his stomach. He is busy preparing contingency plans in case his family doesn't make it home. He pulls out his phone and re-watches the video, analyzing it. He recognizes a few of the bangers from seeing them on the streets. All those weapons they ain't never had this much firepower before. They got them for him. He lets out a deep sigh; he knows it's a trap. He turns off the video.

There are ten minutes left. He calls his mom again, and she quickly answers.

"Where you at?" He blurts out.

"We got caught up in a traffic jam. I don't know what's going on. I think it's an accident or something with all these police around. I can't say how long we are going to be stuck."

"They are not going to blow up pops church. I got about seven minutes left. I'm doing it." He starts down the stairs, headed to the backyard.

"Wait, Sage!" Stephon yells, "That church is just a building. It's not worth dying over!"

"It's not just about the church, it's about respect. Q needs to learn some. Mom, get there when you can." He hangs up

Stuck in traffic, barely moving, Sydney is trying to develop an idea. She unbuckles her seatbelt, gets out, and runs around the front of the car. "You're driving."

Stephon is confused as she approaches his door, "What are you doing?"

"Get out, and you drive. I might be able to link up with Sage while we are stuck in traffic. "I need to be as relaxed as possible, without any outside disturbances. Don't turn on the radio, and go slowly."

Stephon gets out, and they switch places. She lets down her seat. "Alright, here I go," as she closes her eyes.

Sage has changed into the Blac Angel and is in the backyard, about to take flight. He shoots straight up to the sky. The church is five minutes away from the house. Normally, it takes 5 to 10 minutes to get there by car. In the air, he can get there in less than a minute. *I need to get up high to see what the setup is*

The church is situated at the corner of Camden Avenue and Dartmouth Street. It features an old-school red brick design with a steeple on the left. Three steps lead up to the arched red wooden doors beneath the steeple, with a wheelchair ramp on the right side for accessibility. To the right, on a small patch of grass, there's a sign that reads: New Beginning Methodist Church, Rev. Stephon Reed, Pastor. The parking lot at the back has three vehicles, and Q's Suburban is parked across the street in front of the church. Black Angel circles high above, scouting the scene without being seen. Sensing the time pressure, he swoops down and lands in front of the church. Two-armed bangers stand guard with ARs at the door; he quickly sprays his razor-sharp feathers to incapacitate them. Behind him, across the street, Q's Suburban looms, its dark silhouette contrasting against the urban backdrop. Black Angel swiftly turns and unleashes a barrage of sharp feathers toward the driver's side, smashing through the windows with a thunderous crash and causing the front and rear tires to deflate with sickening hisses. He then investigates the back hatch for any hidden grenades; surprisingly, it's empty. His frustration mounting, he forcefully slams the hatch shut, shattering the rear glass. Confidently, he struts across the street, his wings vanishing as he enters the church, where four bangers with AR-15s guard the door. Q is at the pulpit shouting to Blac Angel, "I didn't think you had the balls to show up, Big Saint." The bangers lower their weapons.

Blac Angel walks down the aisle. In the pews are twenty or so bangers, drinking and smoking weed, disrespecting the sanctuary. They are all watching him as he walks up to Q. Blac Angel looks around cautiously, assessing the situation.

"You good, don't worry about them; they just a few friends I invited." Q yells to him from behind his father's wooden pulpit. Sitting in the pastor's chairs behind him are four more bangers in all-black clothing holding AR-15s. Seeing Q standing there in his father's spot pisses him off.

"Big Saint! Look at you, dawg! How in the hell did this happen?"

Blac Angel ignores the question and walks to the stairs.

Q puts his right hand up to stop him at the stairs. "That's far enough, Big Saint!" All four bangers quickly stand up and draw down on him. He stops at the stairs and looks up at Q.

He attempts to control his anger building up inside, “Blac Angel! Big Saint doesn’t exist anymore.”

“Big Saint!” Q retorts mockingly. “No matter what costume you put on or what you call yourself, you're always going to be that little bitch who needed Kong to have his back.”

I’m here, son. Sydney relays to him.

Cool, but I’m good. He replies to her.

Twenty-something gang-bangers surrounding you with army guns, everything is not good. She relays back.

“I know you didn’t call me here to talk. What do you want?” Blac Angel asks.

“It’s simple, you mess with mines, I mess with yours, you leave me alone, I leave you alone. I know your secret, Blac Angel! I know your people. Soon the world is going to know!”

“You threatening my family now? This is between us. Now you crossed a line. The 187s are going down.” He responds defiantly.

An uneasy silence settles over the building as all the bangers rise to their feet, systematically racking their weapons.

Something’s about to happen! She warns.

“If we can’t get along, let’s get it on!” Q hurries away to his right, making a circular hand motion, signaling them to get it going. Two bodyguards with shotguns quickly follow behind him as he leaves.

Suddenly, all the bangers descended upon him fiercely, their AR-15s and shotguns with deadly intent. He whirled around, eyes widening in terror as he took in the chaos, dozens of weapons trained relentlessly on him. The bangers on the altar also surged forward, abruptly tightening as they closed in rapidly, bearing down with menacing hostility.

We need to get out of here now. Sydney relays to him.

His wings unfurl with a majestic spread, glistening in the dim light, as a powerful blast from a hidden banger in the rear ignites. The explosive force propels him forward for a moment, but it also triggers a deadly chain reaction. Gunfire explodes from every direction, a relentless hail of bullets erupts, the sharp crack of AR-15 rounds, and the thudding impact of shotgun shells. The deafening barrage rips into his flesh, tearing through muscle and bone. He drops to his knees, reacting instinctively. He folds his expansive wings tightly around himself, forming a makeshift shield against the onslaught of deadly projectiles, each bullet pinging and ricocheting off his feathers. In his protective cocoon, the cross lights up. The *wounds* on his body began to glow with a white light shining from within, with the bullets being dispelled from his body, and the wounds start too instantly close up. After they are healed, the cross light slowly dims.

As they continue firing at him, Sydney tells him, "*You need to blast straight up and spray feathers like you are a tornado slicing and dicing everything down there.*

"Alright, let's do it!" He erupts off the ground with explosive force, shooting up quickly until he hovers about sixty feet in the air, just beneath the high ceiling of the church. He spins wildly like an enormous, frantic fidget spinner, feathers burst outward in all directions, scattering across the hallowed space. The sharp, barbed feathers slash into the bodies of the armed bangers below, tearing through their clothing and slicing into their weapons, causing them to break apart. He is spinning so fast that he deflects incoming bullets effortlessly, turning him into a blurred, spinning barrier of defense. The faster he spins, the more difficult it becomes for the gunfire to find its mark, and he's gradually taking significantly less fire as the assault progresses. *"It's working, don't stop,"* she urgently relays to him.

No problem, I can do this all day. He spins for another 30 seconds. The shooting had stopped twenty seconds earlier, but he kept spinning to make sure not one banger survived.

He slowly descends back to the floor and can still see some of the bangers moving, injured, and hear them moaning. He surveys the scene, rows of lifeless bodies sprawled across the pews, the shattered glass shards scattered across the floor, torn fabric and splintered wood littering the wreckage of the pews. The once pristine carpet is now ripped and stained, bearing the scars of chaos. It looks like a bomb went off inside it.

Man, I messed up Dad's church.

This is not on you; this is their fault. We still need to find Q.

Blac Angel walks up to the altar and goes to the left, retracing Q's path. The left leads back to the sanctuary. On the right is a small hallway with rooms on both sides.

Do you think he is still here? He asks

I don't know, but we need to check every room.

He creeps cautiously down the hall. At ten feet away is a door. He approaches it, slowly reaches out with his left hand, and checks the knob. The door is locked. He pops the lock and opens it. It is a small storage room filled with tables and chairs. He shuts it and continues his search. The next room is on the right, five feet away. Blac Angel opens it and finds an empty closet. He is getting a little frustrated,

I don't think he's here. He relays to Sydney.

Out of nowhere, a door behind slams open. Before he can turn around, a banger slashes him on his back.

The cut is not deep. It runs from his lower right back to his upper left. Blac Angel struggles to turn around to face his adversary. Much to his surprise, it's Shady. He is dressed in the same black tactical gear as Q and wears dark-tinted goggles. He grips a black-bladed fighting knife in his right hand using a defensive backhand hold.

"Give me what you got, Blac Angel. Shady sneers at him, condensing. HE then rushes, pushing him into a wall and throwing a right-hand hook with his knife. He swiftly strikes Blac Angel, cutting him horizontally across his upper chest. He then swings back with his backhand, cutting him once again close to the same area.

Laughing, he states, "Death by a thousand cuts."

He throws another right-hand hook with his knife hand. This time, Blac Angel blocks it with his left hand as they struggle. Shady counter punches to his exposed right ribs with his left hand. When Blac Angel goes to block, Shady follows with his right to Blac Angel's face. He then throws a left, which Blac Angel blocks with his right and follows with two straight knees to Shady's right ribcage. He swiftly follows up with two quick punches to Shady's face, causing him to fall into the wall. Shady recovers quickly and charges at Blac Angel, attempting to throw another right cross with his knife hand. It is blocked again by Blac Angel. Shady lets the knife go, and it drops smoothly into his left hand, and he stabs Blac Angel on his right side. Shady then spins around and flips Blac Angel over his right shoulder. He then lunges down at Blac Angel, attempting to stab him in the heart. Blac Angel catches his wrist, holding the knife, grabs and flips him fifteen down the hall, crashing into a door.

You need to get out of here; he's too good. She tells him.

I ain't running.

Shady pops back up and comes at him. She messages Blac Angel *I'm gonna flash-blind him, and when he's dazed, you knock him out, and we get the hell out of here.*

Shady moves cautiously as the cross explodes in a blinding flash of intense white light. Despite the sudden burst, Shady remains unharmed, his dark goggles protecting his eyes.

Smiling, he tells Blac Angel, "You gonna have to do better than that. When you are on a mission, you always recon your enemy."

Shady unexpectedly throws a right cross, then a left, and finally an uppercut to Blac Angel's abdomen, all landing with perfect precision.

Suddenly, Q appears unexpectedly behind Blac Angel and shouts loudly, "Go to hell, Big Saint!" before firing his 12-gauge shotgun wildly at him.

Blac Angel, hearing a loud explosion, swiftly turns right and raises his hand to time-shift the incoming shotgun shell. Without delay, he lunges to the right and bursts through the door into the room where Shady was just moments ago. The shotgun shell moves in what seems like slow motion. As it passes, it resumes normal speed, and the deadly shot strikes Shady in the chest and stomach, knocking him into the wall and spraying blood as he collapses, dying instantly.

Q sees this and screams, “Damn Nigga!! You made me kill my boy! Why won’t you die!”

He then takes a grenade from his right cargo pocket, pulls the pin, and rolls it down the hall.

Blac Angel, lying on the floor, forcefully kicks the door shut with his foot. He then unfurls his massive wings. With a powerful thrust, he rockets straight upward, smashing through the ceiling and roof of the building. The structure erupts into chaos and flames beneath him as it collapses and explodes, sending debris flying in all directions.

Looking down from the sky, he sees Q getting into Francisco’s truck on the passenger side. *I got him now.* He relays to Sydney.

Francisco backs the truck up to escape. Blac Angel dives bomb from just above the church’s roof, crashes onto the truck's hood with metal-crunching force. The impact is so intense that the engine crashes to the ground, with all four tires obliterated and instantly flattened.

Blac Angel leaps off the hood of the vehicle with fierce determination, smashing the window with a powerful punch and ripping off the passenger door, which he drops abruptly onto the ground. Using his right hand, he aggressively jerks Q out of the vehicle by gripping his neck, causing Q to gasp for air. Meanwhile, the three bangers quickly open their doors, each emerging swiftly. Q clutches a pistol tightly in his hand, aiming it at Blac Angel's stomach. Just as he pulls the trigger, Blac Angel instinctively snatches the gun from him with a swift motion and forcefully throws it to the ground, smashing it.

Blac Angel yells at the bangers getting out of the truck. “Step off unless anyone wants to die with him! This is between him and me!” All three back away, looking at him. The one in the back passenger seat runs away scared. “Aight, cuz. I got no beef with you.”

Blac Angel is still holding Q by his neck, choking him, slams him against the back door of the truck, and tells him, “You and the 187s are done!”

Q’s gagging as he answers, “Big Saint, you're a bad dude with the superpowers, but deep inside, I still know you, that soft punk Sage Reed. The same little punk Kong had to protect! I don’t know how you got these powers, but without them, you're still Charmin' soft.”

“I don’t need any powers to take care of you!” Blac Angel snaps back.

Q gagging responds, “That’s what you are saying. Prove it! Right here! Right now! Let’s go!”

Sydney relays to him. *You don’t have to do this. You've got nothing to prove to him. Knock him out and let the police take him.*

Yeah, I do. He relays back. *The disrespect ends today.*

Still holding him in a tight chokehold, he forcefully body slams him to the ground, causing Q to lose his breath.

Then he leans down, inches from his face, eyes locking onto his. “Say less! Don’t go anywhere! I will be back!”

His wings formulate, and he flies to the front of the church. As he walks into the church, Sydney relays to him *I don’t agree with you doing this, but know this Blac Angel isn’t the reason you are strong. You are the reason Blac Angel is strong. You are the roots that give Blac Angel his strength. Now take this mf down.*

Stephon’s insides are torn up as tears welled up in his eyes. He wandered through the wreckage of his church, glancing around at the shattered pews, scorched walls, and fallen debris, overwhelmed by the extent of the destruction.

“Dad, I’m so sorry about the damage. I did not know it was going to be this bad.” Blac Angel states.

Stephon shakes his head as he looks around, “That’s not important right now.” He looks at his son and sees all his cuts and bruises. “You alright?”

“Yeah, I’ll be alright. Mom, work your magic.” He raises his arms above his head, and the cuts glow and self-heal.

Stephon shakes his head in amazement, “Boy, will the miracles ever cease?”

“I'm still learning stuff myself. Mom just showed it to me earlier. I don’t have time to talk about it. I need to take care of some unfinished business in the parking lot.”

Blac Angel takes off the cross and gives it to Stephon. He transitions back to Sage.

Sage turns around and walks to the door. Stephon grabs him by his right arm, "Where you going?"

"Me and Q are about to settle this for good."

"Why didn't you do it as Blac Angel?"

"This doesn't concern Blac Angel. He stares at Stephon's hand on his shoulder, "Can you let go of me?"

"Do it as Blac Angel!" Stephon demands.

"Blac Angel can't get me the respect I deserve." He changes to a stressed tone, "Now, please take your hands off."

Stephon glares at his son, sees there is nothing he can say to him, and let's go of his arm. Sage walks to the door without looking back and retorts, "Mom should be here soon. She already knows."

He follows behind Sage, "I can't stand around while my son gets killed."

A crowd of about twenty people gathers around the parking lot, forming a semicircle. All the bangers surround Q as he kneels on his left knee, tying his boot.

Q stands up and motions with both arms for Sage to come over, "Big Saint, you want the respect, come take it!"

Sage slightly shakes his head and swiftly walks over. He instantly throws a right cross that Q blocks with his left, and Q follows with an uppercut to his stomach.

Sage crouches in pain, then Q knees him in the face. He then grabs Sage by the back of his shirt and slings him into the truck's back door. Sage puts out his right foot to block this. He then quickly reverses, spins, and faces Q. Sage throws both arms up, breaking Q's grip. He does a four-punch combo to Q's stomach, then a spinning back kick with his right leg. It lands on Q's left jaw, knocking him back about ten feet.

Sage smiles at him and thinks, *He doesn't have the skills Shady does, thank goodness.*

Q cautiously crouches down and slowly creeps toward Sage.

With Sage's back to the building, Q lunges at him, picks him up, carries him a few yards, and slams him to the ground on his back. Q is on top of him and starts delivering blows to his face. Sage thrust his but off the ground, throwing Q face-first into some old metal garbage cans by the corner of the building.

Q lies in the garbage cans while Sage quickly springs to his feet.

Q struggles to stand as he gets up. He grabs a lid and smashes it into Sage's face, stunning him. He quickly follows it up with a second shot, smashing the lid on top of his head, causing Sage to retreat a few steps. Q then throws the lid at him like a Frisbee, which Sage ducks.

Sage, still dazed, looks at him. "That's how you playin, huh?"

"What's the matter, Big Saint? This is war. Ain't no rules in love and war."

"If that's how you want to do it." He swiftly walks up to him. Q swings at him with a right cross. Sage ducks under the punch, which causes Q to lose his balance. With his left leg, Sage kicks him in the back of the head. He then flips around and kicks him in his chest with his right leg. Q falls to the ground and double-kicks him in the chest when Sage tries to attack him. Sage falls into a banger standing in the crowd. The banger grabs his arms and locks them behind his back. Q goes over and punches him in the face with a right cross, then a left, and then a right uppercut to Sage's stomach. Sage's head drops. He's delirious from the onslaught of punches he's taken. Q walks to him, lifts his chin with his left, and delivers a straight right to his face. Sage's nose and lips are bloodied from the punch, and he collapses, only being held up by the banger, who then lets him drop to the ground. Q picks up Sage's limp body and holds it over his head, yelling, "You really thought you were man enough to take on the King, Big Saint! You got more heart than I thought, too bad you had to die to show it." He then slams him into the pavement face-first.

Everybody in the crowd oohs and ahhs because of the slam. Stephon sees this and turns his head away, walking to the rear. He cannot stand to watch this. Sydney, standing beside him, crouches down and yells to Sage, "Get up, son! You are more man than he will ever be. Get your respect!"

Q glances at her as he approaches and pushes her down, and then flips her the bird. Basking in the moment, he struts around Sage similar to what those wrestlers do on TV. Q crows, "187 run this and always will, today, Elk City! Tomorrow, the world!" As he is boasting, Sage is slowly regaining his strength as Q struts over to him for the kill shot. Sage rolls onto his back, quickly spins his legs to trip Q to the ground, and he ends up on his back. Sage then springs up and jumps onto Q's chest, pressing his right knee against Q's neck. He grabs Q's right arm, using his left arm to try to break Q's right arm. In a panic, pressed by Sage's knee on his neck and the threat of his arm snapping, Q instinctively reaches into his left boot with his left hand, pulls out a knife, and stabs Sage in the lower right back, twisting the blade. He withdraws it and stabs him again, one inch above the original wound.

Sage screams out in agony, and he quickly snaps Q's arm with the adrenaline rush from the pain. With his right hand, he grabs the back of Q's head by the dreadlocks and smashes it into the concrete repeatedly. After the fourth slam, he hears his skull crack, and blood oozes out the back of his head. Q's body goes limp. He is unalived.

Sage collapses on top of him.

Sydney cries out, “Oh my God!! No!!

Sydney and Stephon run over to him. “Let’s get him in the church,” she tells Stephon.

They carefully take Sage off Q and drag him into the church. He stays conscious but is disoriented, eyes fluttering as he winces in pain, the knife still embedded deeply in his back. Tears stream down his face as he struggles to stay alert.

At the church doors, Candace is waiting. Seeing the knife in his back, screamed, “What happened?”

“We don’t have time to talk! We need to get him inside,” Sydney yells. “Get the door.”

Candace opens the door as they drag Sage in and lay him on the back pew.

“Go get the cross,” Sydney yells to Stephon.

He runs to the pulpit, gets it, and gives it to Sydney.

Sydney looks down at Sage and sees the agony he is in. “Here’s your cross.”

He lifts his head, and she places it around his neck.

“I’m taking the knife out now.” This allows him to prepare for the pain of it being pulled out.

She slowly pulls the knife out. The wounds glow and start closing immediately, and he transitions into the Blac

Angel, all healed up. He sits up, and Sydney hugs him, "Thank you, God! I know we have no control when it's our time to go, but you can't keep tempting fate."

He smiles at her, "Come on now, we're a team. Tempting fate is what we do."

Stephon hugs him, "I know we don't always see everything the same, but I can't lose you when we started getting closer. I love you, son."

Candace, stunned, asks incredulously, "So you're the Blac Angel?"

He stands up, smiles, and tells her, "We've got a lot of things to talk about."

Amira is outside, kneeling over Q's limp body, crying, whispering in his ear, "It's not over Blac Angel. I know your secret."

THE END?

ACKNOWLEDGMENTS

Righteous Gangsta Rise of The Blac Angel. This was the most challenging book I'd written so far. Everything about this story was challenging, from his name to the origin story to his powers. This really stretched my imagination. After the Skyy family trilogy, I wanted to step outside my comfort zone and try something different. Hopefully, I succeeded in creating a new superhero. I must thank the following people for making this book possible.

First and most importantly, I need to praise and honor our **Lord and Savior, Jesus, the Son of GOD.** He gave me the strength to push through the difficult times when writing this book. Through him, anything is possible.

My Choctaw brother and collaborator, **Stephen Reid.** We talked about writing a superhero story about six months ago. I wasn't sure how it would happen, but here it is. I would not have been able to do this story without you planting the seed. You gave valuable feedback and input to the story. There would be no Blac Angel without you.

Mr. Frank King put together this incredible book cover. I reached out to him with a cover idea, thinking we could work together on it for a few weeks. Mr. King took the idea and ran with it. The cover was done in less than a week. I appreciate your effort, Mr. King, and I hope we will have the chance to work together again. If anyone is interested in using his services, he can be reached through Facebook DM.

Randy Norris, a fellow Choctaw writer. Your ideas and feedback helped write the book. I have read some of your work. You are very talented; you need to share your gift with the world.

Alyssa Cox, Thank you for reading the first copies and for your insight into this story.

Last but certainly not least, my wife and life partner, **Gayla**. You have been with me for every book. You are exactly what I need when I need it. You give me the space to write and also provide feedback and ideas. Thank you for believing in me.

This book uses religious ideas to tell a story. I apologize if I have offended anyone's religious beliefs. It is not my intention to disrespect any religion.

Thank you for taking the time to read the story. I'm not sure what's next, another **Blac Angel** story. Maybe something new and different, only time will tell. **DM me through Facebook. Please leave a review on Amazon.**

Check out my trilogy on Amazon: **The Last Time, You Never Said Goodbye**, **and Closure.**

My books in Order are available at **erickwilliamsauthor.com**

1. The Last Time

2. You Never Said Goodbye

3. Closure

4. Righteous Gangsta: Rise of the Blac Angel

5. The Wendigos'Prey

6. Unfinished Love

www.ingramcontent.com/pod-product-compliance
Lightning Source LLC
LaVergne TN
LVHW050625100826
845148LV00011B/1735

* 9 7 9 8 9 8 7 5 4 7 0 7 6 *